RODGERS

Island of peril

Books by Raboo Rodgers

Magnum Fault
The Rainbow Factor
Island of Peril

Island of Peril

ISLAND OF PERIL

RABOO RODGERS

Houghton Mifflin Company
Boston, 1987

Library of Congress Cataloging-in-Publication Data

Rodgers, Raboo
Island of peril.

Summary: On a Caribbean island, two teenagers find
their lives in danger when they uncover a smuggling
operation involving stolen Mayan art treasures.
[1. Smuggling — Fiction. 2. West Indies—Fiction. 3. Islands—Fiction]   I. Title.
PZ7.R6157Is   1987   [Fic]   86-27544
ISBN 0-395-43082-8

Printed in the United States of America

P 10 9 8 7 6 5 4 3 2 1

for Rebecca

*And with very special appreciation to
Phil Sadler, who spreads the good word*

Island of Peril

One

The night and sea were black off the bow of the sailing yacht, but the radar screen in the well-fitted-out pilot house showed a large green smear, indicating the mass of Sabado's shoreline dead ahead.

The Frenchman switched off the autopilot and spun the wheel, turning the vessel into the wind, allowing her to roll with the swells. He would have to lie off-shore until daybreak, when the treacherous waters of rocks and coral heads that surrounded the island could be safely navigated by a deep-water boat.

The Frenchman started forward to furl the flapping sails, and he did not see the other smear of green, a small one, entering quickly from the right side of the radar screen.

From below decks, his wife shouted that the rolling was making her sick. In the forward cabin, a young dog stirred only briefly in its restful sleep, the change in the boat's movement not sufficient to awaken it completely.

On deck, the Frenchman wrestled with the big mainsail, and then suddenly he threw himself against the boom, clutching it in horror.

At first, he saw only the hideous face, the curl of horn and fang and claw, as the demonic figure emerged from the blackness. The grotesque apparition seemed to ride through the air above the dark sea, and it came swiftly, heading directly for the sailboat.

For an instant, the Frenchman thought the eighteen hours he had spent on watch had made him delirious and he was beginning to hallucinate. Then he saw water folding white from the point of a bow beneath the belly of the demon, and he knew it was all too real.

Leading the black hull of the vessel that carried it, the evil face of the demon climbed over the sailboat's gunwale and snapped through her starboard lifeline near the bow. The yacht yielded, her hull splintering, and went down hard on her side.

The sailboat's main boom struck the sea, and the Frenchman catapulted over it, landing in the water, trapped in the folds of the sail. When the yacht righted, he was lifted in a sling formed by the sail and boom and swung to the side of the boat. Pulling himself over the toe rail, he crawled onto the deck just in time to see the high pointed stern of the horrible vessel disappear over the swells into the night.

He had never seen anything like it and had no idea what it was. It had had no sails, and there had been no engine noise, yet the dark craft had moved fast enough to make teeth as it came and to lay a white wake as it left.

Now there was other noise. The Frenchman's wife was yelling again, screaming this time. Scrambling to the companionway, he found her in the main cabin. In her night clothes, she stood in water that was already thigh deep and rising.

"We're going to die! We're going to die!" she wailed.

"Get topside!" the Frenchman shouted and raced for the inflatable lifeboat lashed to the top of the deckhouse.

The water was nearly to the yacht's gunwales as they shoved away. With his wife huddled in the bow, the Frenchman worked at getting the outboard started.

"We're going to die!" she repeated.

"No," he said, trying to give her an assurance he did not feel. "We'll be on Sabado ten minutes after I get this engine to run."

"You ran us into a rock!" she said accusingly.

"No, we were run down by a . . . by something . . ." The Frenchman shuddered. Fear slashed at him again, and he had to fight back panic. "I don't know what it was!"

His wife, distraught, missed the quiet horror in his voice. "A boat? I did not hear a boat."

The Frenchman pulled repeatedly on the starter rope, trying to coax the stubborn outboard to life.

They were drifting away from the foundering yacht, gradually losing sight of it in the dark as the sea began to wash over the deck.

"My jewelry! My diamond brooch!" the woman gasped in another seizure of dismay. "I've lost it all!"

"Where's the dog?" the Frenchman asked, suddenly remembering the cuddly young animal that he had purchased as a gift for his wife two days earlier in Pointe-à-Pitre, Guadeloupe.

"Oh dear!" she replied, her voice with an edge of guilt. "I didn't want him bothering me, so I — I put him in the front. I forgot about him. The poor thing. Maybe we should look for him."

The Frenchman grunted. He saw the tall mast going straight down, like a stiff string of spaghetti sucked into the mouth of the sea. It was too bad about the dog, he thought. But there was no way they were going to hang around and look for him. Not with that *thing* out there.

Choke on, another pull of the starter rope brought the outboard motor sputtering to life. The Frenchman twisted the throttle, and the engine ran smoothly.

* * *

The dog came awake at the moment of impact — his impact with the edge of the bulkhead on the opposite side of the cabin. When he regained his senses, he smelled the sea water flooding in, but it was not until he suddenly found himself swimming in the narrow confines of the cabin and clawing for refuge that he became concerned.

For long seconds he swam in circles, haphazardly

4

bumping off the sides and bulkheads, pawing at floating debris — books, a pillow, a plastic file box. The water rose rapidly, carrying him up to meet the ceiling, and he swam with frantic strokes. He caught a whiff of outside air, and he struggled, trying to reach it.

With the space above him shrinking to inches, he heard the last of the air being belched from the doomed yacht, forcing away the smell of the outside. A moment later, his head knocked against the ribs that supported the top of the deckhouse, and then the water swallowed him.

Kicking and thrashing, he fought blindly, wildly. His claws skittered against the smooth, polished wood of the sinking yacht's interior, and then his rear paws found an edge. He thrust up and away.

He did not strike the ceiling again. Instead, he shot up through the open deck hatch in the center of the cabin and rose in a froth of bubbles, free of the yacht's lonely death fall to the bottom of the sea.

His head broke through the surface, and he breathed the cool night air. Around him, the swells were like black, undulating hills.

The only sound he heard was the receding noise of an outboard motor.

Two

When Jeri entered the portable building that served as the harbor project's on-site headquarters, Mr. Fitzgerald, the company clerk, was the only one inside.

"Good morning, Miss Collins," he said with a tone of respect she wished people wouldn't use. It was the inevitable result of her being the boss's daughter. "Your father's out talking with the dredge crew, but he should be coming back in any time now. I'll be glad to radio him for you if you like."

"No, I've got a few minutes, so I'll just wait," she replied, walking to the window behind her father's desk.

Shielding her eyes against the morning glare, she spotted her father's launch about two hundred meters out in Humpback Bay. It was tied to a barge that supported the giant dragline.

Fitzgerald felt compelled to make conversation. "Did you hear about the French couple in the yacht?"

"It would be impossible not to have heard about it. It's almost the only thing people are talking about on the island radios. They said they were run down by a 'devil ship.' "

Fitzgerald snorted, scoffing at the report. "That's all these islanders need — rumors of some 'devil ship.' They're already so superstitious that the laborers refuse to work on any of the last five days of the year, just because the local soothsayers claim those are evil days."

Jeri continued to gaze at the view. Humpback Bay was ringed by lushly vegetated volcanic formations, the largest of which gave the bay its name. Jeri had been on the Caribbean island for nearly four weeks with her father, and she was still awed at every turn by the island's incredible and rugged beauty.

"Well, that's the same time as their Carnival," she said.

"Five days of worthlessness, if you ask me," Fitzgerald replied. "Of course, once this deep-water port is finished and some tourists start coming in here, Carnival might not be such a bad idea. Anything that'll put some money into this economy couldn't be all bad. The only thing that's kept the island going till now has been all the stealing they've done from this company. Up until your father came, you couldn't turn your back for a second without someone stealing everything right out from under you."

"What happened to them?" she asked. "The French couple on the yacht, I mean. Are they still here?"

"Matta was in here earlier," Fitzgerald said, meaning Joe Matta, the young Sabadoan who was chief of the island's constabulary and customs department. "He said the woman was throwing a fit, demanding that her husband get her back to 'civilization' immediately. Matta said he radioed the airport at Martinique for them and had a chartered seaplane sent over."

Jeri saw her father, followed by Brocker, the big foreman, board the launch and shove away from the barge. Cutting a furrow in the water, the boat came toward the small wooden dock behind the office. In a movement that was automatic and routine, Vernon Collins threw the wheel over and cut the throttle. The craft sidled to the end of the dock and died there. Brocker dropped the mooring line over the piling.

Walking up the dock, the engineer wrinkled his nose affectionately at his daughter in the window. He came into the office talking to Brocker.

"I've decided we're going to go ahead and do it," Collins said. "All the sand and much of the rock we take from the channel or the bay will go into the concrete for the quays and pier."

"It sure is a lot easier to barge all that to sea, and just scoop the sand we need from the beach," Brocker replied. "Also there's a lot of other stuff in the sand that comes off the bottom, Mr. Collins — weeds and crabs and fish and stuff we don't want in the concrete."

"I know. That's why we'll clean it first. We'll even screen it if we have to. We're not here to destroy the island's ecology."

When she was alone with her father, Jeri said, "Well, you certainly seem like the man who has everything under control."

Collins shook his head and groaned, but good-naturedly. Then he frowned and looked serious. "I've been here a month, and it's taken nearly all that time just to get this outfit to a point where it can *begin* to get a little work done. I can't believe it was so fouled up. SeaCon's been on this island over a year — the job was originally scheduled to take only two years — and hardly anything has been accomplished."

"Well, that's why SeaCon hired you to take charge — so you can fix all that," Jeri said with what had become a kind of casual faith in her father's abilities.

"Yeah? Well, don't buy any of their stock yet," he cautioned.

"I missed you at breakfast," she said.

"You slept too late."

"You left too early. Anja said you were gone before the sun was up."

Collins shook his head. "For an old woman, Anja is as alert as a cat. I thought I got away without anyone hearing."

"I thought I'd stop by and see if there was anything you'd like me to do before I go to the library," Jeri said.

"Still reading about the island?" he asked.

9

"Anything that I can find, which isn't much. The library — well," she said with a laugh, "the library is kind of small. And apparently there's been very little written about the history of Sabado, anyway. But for a number of years there was a local newspaper, a weekly, and the library has most of the old copies, which are pretty interesting. They give a really colorful look at the way the people lived. I've been going through those."

"Good," her father said, pleased. "Anything you do that will enable us to have a better understanding of Sabado and its people has the potential of helping this port project go more smoothly. I would say your efforts are well spent."

Jeri smiled. "Finding out about Sabado requires about the same effort as having a fun vacation does."

"So, vacate," he said, squeezing her affectionately again and then pushing her away. "I have work to do. Oh boy, do I have work to do!"

Three

Guiding the Land Rover through the narrow streets of Rotole, the small coastal town that held most of Sabado's small population, Jeri again experienced the feeling of pleasure that living on the island had been giving her with such frequency.

Not only was Sabado of staggering beauty, boasting towering peaks, dense primeval rain forests, and beaches of black volcanic sand that twinkled with flecks of pure quartz, it was also a very hospitable place. There may have been some trouble with stealing at SeaCon before her father came, but Sabado's people were the warmest and most open to strangers that she had ever known. As she drove by, children laughed and waved, and colorfully dressed men and women smiled at her in genuine friendliness.

For a moment, Jeri wondered about the wisdom of

the decision made by the consortium of countries that were underwriting SeaCon's construction of the deep-water port. A port would change the island forever. But as Fitzgerald had said, the local economy was almost nonexistent. A deep-water port would enable the big cruise ships to begin stopping at the out-of-the-way island, and the money from the tourist trade was badly needed for schools and health-care facilities and generally to improve the islanders' standard of living.

The library will be able to use some of that money, too, Jeri thought, as she walked up the narrow path from where she parked the Land Rover on the street.

Built against the very edge of the high sea wall, the small wooden building with sagging wrap-around porch and sagging floors, was dwarfed by the most magnificent banyan tree Jeri had ever seen. The giant tree had spread out over the grounds and library, dropping shoots from its limbs and establishing secondary trunks, until both tree and library looked like a single structural mass.

Inside, wide barren spaces on many of the shelves testified to the scant money available for the library's budget. The young librarian smiled timidly at Jeri and nodded with pleasure when Jeri indicated that she was returning to continue going over back issues of the now-defunct *Voice*.

More gossip sheet than newspaper, the *Voice* had chronicled such events as who had been the most intoxicated at Maxine's Bar on Saturday night, births and deaths, visits by relatives from neighboring islands, and the substance of the local preacher's Sunday sermon. Having read several years of past issues already, Jeri had developed a feel for what the paper reported, and she came across a headline that she almost expected: DEVIL SPIRIT EATS WOMAN'S DOG.

The gist of the story was that a woman living near the north end of the island had awakened in the night to the barking of her several dogs and gone outside to witness a "much horrible devil" that by her description was apparently half man and half serpent. "And there were horns on the shoulders and a snake's body coming out and curling all over from where the awful neck thing should be. I saw with my own eyes this snake head as it bit at my little dog that was too slow to get itself away, and the snake head swallowed up my dog before the devil did then rise up and fly away into the night."

Jeri smiled, amused. Regularly, on the order of about every six months' worth of newspapers, she had come across a story like this. Invariably, some sort of horrible monster had made an appearance near the north end of the island where the "Ancients" had lived, and just as invariably, the monster ate something, usually a chicken, a cat, or a dog. Also invariably, the story was told by someone who "wished not to have their name be known, should they suffer ridicule of an unwarranted nature."

Jeri had her own ideas about the stories. They were too pat, too regular. She suspected that they were merely a ploy by the *Voice*'s editor to sell more papers by taking advantage of the islanders' belief in the supernatural. The stories all had such a familiar ring that she had little doubt that they were made up, and probably by the same person. Sure that she would come across another one, she went on reading.

A few minutes later the librarian cleared her throat softly beside Jeri and held out a folder. "I wondered if you would be interested in this," she said. "It seems to be a study about Sabado, written by an American man of academics. I found it among other items which Mrs. Dibb was cataloging before she died." Mrs. Dibb had been the previous librarian and had died a few months before Jeri came to the island.

Thanking her, Jeri took the folder, which contained a copy of a graduate student's thesis written more than twenty years earlier in partial fulfillment of the requirements for a master's degree from the University of Texas Department of Anthropology. The author's name was Winston Moore, and his thesis bore the title "A Survey of Evidence Supporting the Mayan Origins of Early Sabadoan Culture."

The writing was dry and academic, but Jeri found the paper interesting, nonetheless. Its introduction summarized the small amount that was known of Sabado's history. The island had been discovered by Columbus in 1492, on a Saturday morning; hence its name, Sabado, which was Spanish for Saturday. At that time it was inhabited by the fierce Carib Indians, who were eradicated over the ensuing decades by the Spaniards' muskets. In the following centuries, the island was claimed by almost every European power — the French, Dutch, Spanish, and English — and was

14

then repopulated by a mixture of peoples from throughout the Caribbean.

The theme of the paper, however, dealt with the ruins at the north end of the island. The author believed they dated from before A.D. 800, and he went into great detail to show what he perceived to be similarities between the glyphs and paintings of the Sabadoan ruins with those found in the ruins of Mayan civilizations of Central America. Even to Jeri's untrained eye, the sketches the student anthropologist had made of the figures from the two cultures were strikingly alike, especially in the depictions of the heads of humans and animals. The main difference that the paper noted was in the presence of a large, double-ended "war canoe" among the Sabadoan glyphs, a representation the author of the paper said was not found in mainland Mayan ruins.

The existence of this vessel was the main support of the paper's theory of how a splinter group of Mayans could have crossed hundreds of miles of open sea to settle on an obscure island, where the evidence indicated they lived for nearly two hundred years "before most likely being overrun and massacred by raiding parties of Carib Indians."

The author lamented the fact that over the years the small Sabadoan ruins had been so ravaged by looters that anthropological evidence was severely limited, handicapping his study. It was his opinion that a well-organized dig would reveal additional ruins; however, he cautioned that such an undertaking not be attempted until the Sabadoan government had both the

15

means and will to secure the site in perpetuity. Otherwise, the inevitable looting would result in the permanent loss of these priceless cultural treasures.

It was almost noon before Jeri reached the end of the thesis, and she was excited by what she had read. Turning the pages of the index, she found a detailed map of the location and entrance to the Sabadoan ruins. She thought there would be more, a drawing of the inside perhaps, but then noticed small bits of paper behind the clasps of the binder. The final few pages had been torn out.

"There seem to be a few pages of this missing," Jeri said, taking the paper to the librarian. "You wouldn't know where they are, would you?"

The young woman shook her head, embarrassed that she had given Jeri something incomplete. "I am sorry, but I am still finding things. If I should come across them . . ."

"Oh, that's okay," Jeri replied. "Even without them, it's really interesting to me, and I'm very grateful that you let me look at it. I wonder, could I take this with me and make a copy of it at my father's office?"

The librarian looked thoughtful for a moment and said, "It is reference material, and Mrs. Dibb never permitted reference materials to be taken from the library." Then she smiled warmly. "But of course I am in charge now. I would be happy for you to borrow it."

"Thank you so much," Jeri said, heading for the door. "I'll have it back within an hour. I promise."

Four

Shielding his eyes from the glare, Ben watched the eight-foot hammerhead glide past the stern again. The big shark banked and studied him with one of its small beady eyes. Then, as it had done numerous times over the past several hours, it slid into the depths and disappeared.

Ben leaned back in the cockpit and looked up at *Trike*'s limp sails. He sighed. In almost four months of cruising the waters of the Gulf and Caribbean, the trimaran had never been so absolutely becalmed. Not a breath of air had stirred since before dawn, and the big genoa and mainsail hung lifelessly above a sea so flat and still that it looked oily.

He had already taken the noon fix with his sextant and figured his position, and with that done, Ben felt the creeping return of boredom and loneliness, the twin conditions that were the nemesis of all single-handed sailors. The searing heat of midday made him long to go over the side, but the frequent appearance of the hammerhead had ruled out even that.

People who grew up on the Mississippi River weren't used to swimming with sharks, he thought, trying to inject a little humor into the breezeless day.

In *Trike*'s small galley, Ben looked over the selection of canned goods and shook his head dismally. His mouth watered for anything but what he had. Opening a can of beans and franks, he sucked the juice from one of the franks and carried it topside, where he slipped it on the hook of the hand line and dropped it from the stern.

There were other fish down there. If the hammerhead would give him a chance, maybe he could get one of them.

He sat, waiting for a fish or the wind, whichever came first. He thought about how far he was from home now. Although it was the zigzag course of a sailboat, he had logged nearly three thousand miles since leaving the mouth of the Mississippi. He felt pride in that, but at moments like this he wondered if it was really worth it.

The fishing line snapped taut, hard, at the cleat but didn't break, so he knew it wasn't the hammerhead. Still, whatever it was was bigger than a Mississippi largemouth. That was for sure. The fish bucked and fought as Ben took in line.

Veering toward the boat, the fish changed tactics

and began coming up fast, breaking water fifty feet away. It was a king mackerel, at least forty pounds of tasty meat.

Well, the fishing isn't as fickle as the wind, Ben thought, bracing his back and taking in line hand-over-hand from the tiring fish.

Then he saw the dark shadow, like the blade of a knife, slicing upward from the depths.

Fifteen feet from the boat, the water suddenly roiled, and instantly the line went limp. The hammerhead, still gulping, turned at the side of the boat and went back to get the rest of what remained attached to the hook.

"Damn you!" Ben shouted and snatched the line as hard as he could.

The head and forward third of the king mackerel came aboard in a splatter of red blood against the white deck. In one swift bite, the hammerhead had razored away all of the fish below the first dorsal fin, but there were still several pounds of edible meat attached to the head. Ben set about salvaging what he could of his catch.

When the hammerhead passed again, Ben cursed it and shook his fist at it. The shark came so close to the boat that it would have been an easy shot with a speargun, but Ben figured he would only end up losing his spear if he tried it.

Dorsal fin slicing through the surface, the hammerhead circled tightly in search of more of the fish. When Ben glanced up again, he thought he saw something farther out, beyond the shark. Two hundred feet to starboard, an object appeared to be floating, bobbing sluggishly on the glassy surface of the sea.

Stepping into the cockpit, Ben reached inside the companionway and brought out his binoculars.

The object was not easily identifiable, and at first he thought it might be a wad of floating seaweed. Then, steadying himself against the corner of the cabin, Ben began to make out detail through the glasses. Whatever the thing was, it was black and looked like sodden wool.

One thing he had never seen in the Caribbean was a seal, but there was a small snout and what looked like whiskers —

"It's a dog!" he exclaimed suddenly, hardly believing it. But in another moment he was convinced. It *was* a dog — or at least the carcass of one.

Then Ben detected faint movement, no more than a slight stirring motion, but he was sure he saw it.

"Holy — it's alive!"

But there was other movement that wasn't so faint. The hammerhead had increased its prowl area, circling farther out from the boat, and already it had picked up the promise of a new scent.

Scrambling onto the deck, Ben scooped up the pieces of king mackerel and threw the head in the direction of the shark. The hammerhead reacted immediately and turned back. Double rows of teeth gaping open, the big shark rolled under the sinking fish head and swallowed it as if it was no more substantial than a gumdrop.

Ben threw more chunks of fish, luring the shark back to the boat. Then he ran to the bow and flung the remaining pieces as far away from the direction of the dog as he could.

Snatching at cleated halyards, Ben dropped all sails to the deck, letting them lie where they fell. He got the nylon sea anchor from beneath a cockpit seat, tied its line to a winch, and tossed it from the stern to slow *Trike*'s drift if the wind came up while he was out.

Pausing to make sure the shark was still distracted by the chum, Ben removed the tiny dinghy from its tie-downs and eased it into the pocket of water between the center and starboard hulls.

He rowed slowly, regularly, trying not to send an alarm signal to the shark. Looking over his shoulder, Ben held his course on the dog and gradually closed the distance between them. As he neared the small animal, he began to doubt that it was alive after all. Then he saw the movement again, a barely perceptible stirring.

Glare, reflected by the white of *Trike*'s triple hulls and collapsed sails, obscured the hammerhead's position, and Ben's uneasiness went up a notch. When he saw the shark again, his heart leaped up in his throat. It was coming straight for him.

Gripping the oars tightly, Ben braced for the collision, but the big hammerhead slid beneath the dinghy and ghosted past without making contact. Ben shuddered at the size of the beast. It was several times the mass of him and the dinghy combined. He dipped the oars again and corrected his course for the dog.

21

The little animal's eyes were glassy and unresponsive. Its hindquarters were angled down, and the only movement it made was feeble, the remnants of swimming strokes with its front paws. The small dog had been in the water for a long time, fighting for its life, and now it was all but finished.

Already having made one curious pass at the dog, the hammerhead was circling back. Ben saw the shark begin the wagging motion that indicated it was moving in for the kill. At the last minute, the hammerhead veered, rolling water and passing so close that it left the dog turning in its turbulence.

Ben slapped the water with the blade of an oar, making a sound like a firecracker, but the shark was unaffected. The monster turned, coming back for the kill.

Ben pulled harder on the oars, shooting the dinghy toward the dog. He was vaguely aware that he was risking his own life for an animal that was already more dead than alive. If he got knocked into the water, the hammerhead would eat him as incidentally as it was going to eat the dog.

The shark and Ben converged on the dog simultaneously.

The hammerhead wagged and rolled, turning up an open manhole ringed with teeth.

Ben lifted an oar and with both hands jammed it down toward the shark's mouth as hard as he could.

There was a crack like a rifle shot. The water exploded, and the dinghy rocked backward. Ben grabbed the sides and held on.

When the shark's wake settled, Ben was still sitting squarely in the seat. The oar had been bitten off cleanly, and he held only the shaft in his hands.

In the water and almost against the dinghy's gunwale, the dog floated, oblivious to what was going on around him. With one hand Ben lifted the animal by the scruff of his neck and deposited him into the dinghy at his feet. The dog collapsed there and did not move.

Paddling back to *Trike* with one oar, Ben kept a wary eye on the shark. The hammerhead continued to circle, but the dinghy's shape was confusing to the limited programs of its small brain, and the awesome sea predator did not attack.

Ben laid the dog on the floor inside *Trike*'s main cabin and examined him. There were no broken bones or any other evidence of injury, but he was suffering from exposure.

Lying on his side, the dog was motionless, and then he began vomiting, throwing up large quantities of sea water. Ben held him in a more upright position to keep him from strangling himself. The dog continued to throw up until the tight, swollen belly became slack and sunken in. Now, for the first time, the dog showed some awareness. He rolled his eyes and looked at Ben. Ben thought he saw the nub of a tail wag.

Ben flushed the floor with salt water and brought a small cup of fresh water from the galley. The dog struggled for it, lapping eagerly.

"Easy now, black dog, don't go and make yourself sick all over again," Ben said soothingly.

Ben waited several minutes before giving him more water and took nearly an hour of allowing only small amounts before he had given him all he wanted. Rehydrated, the dog seemed to feel better. He stood up shakily and looked around and looked at Ben, then sat down and burped several times, an expression of relief spreading over his whiskered face as his stomach deflated again.

Ben opened a can of beef hash and put two small spoonfuls into a bowl. The dog went for it immediately, wolfing it down. Licking his lips, he looked up at Ben and wagged his nub of a tail more vigorously.

Ben laughed. "You sure like that stuff better than I do, black dog. I guess it would be okay to give you a little more."

Ben was still below with the dog, when he heard the scuffing noise of collapsed sails being pushed about the deck and rigging by air. Topside, he found *Trike* turning in a stiffening breeze.

Under mainsail and jib, *Trike* got up on a reach, her windward hull light on the surface. With the kind of speed that only a multihull can steal from the wind, the trimaran cut a swift path across the Caribbean.

Ben looked at his watch and had a happy thought. If he could hold this pace, he would make Sabado before dark.

Belowdecks, Black Dog snuggled into a corner of Ben's bunk. Fed and dried and comfortable, he lapsed into a sleep so deep that he didn't even wonder if the water was going to come in on this boat, too.

Five

"Oh, Anja, you know that's not true," Jeri said, laughing softly. "You really can't expect me to believe in such things, can you?"

"You best listen to me, child," Anja said, firmly leveling her finger at Jeri. "I did not reach to this age by refusing in my heart the signs and warnings of the spirits."

Jeri checked the contents of her rucksack one last time before buckling the straps. The peanut-butter sandwich and candy bar were the most essential items, but the Thermos of ice-cold limeade that Anja had made from three plump Sabadoan limes was what would be most welcome. When she looked up, Jeri saw the hard, serious expression on the old woman's leathery face, and she almost wished she hadn't told Anja where she was going.

"I don't believe in jombies, Anja. It's just not in me to believe such things."

"Then you best find it and put it in there to believe, child," Anja replied, wagging her finger at her again. "You go to the devil place of the Ancients, and I say it's the same that you ask not to come back again. Lord be with you, child, but even the Lord walks wide around such evil place."

"I'll be careful, Anja, I promise," Jeri said, squeezing her arm affectionately.

But Anja was not to be mollified. The spry old woman followed Jeri out the door, across the wide wooden porch, and down the steps. "The rich Frenchman was much a careful person, too, child, and the devil came across the water all the same to sink the man's boat. It did this, and then it *ate the baby of that man's wife!*"

Jeri stopped in her tracks between the giant ferns, taller than a man, that lined the walk. "*What?*" She couldn't believe what she was hearing. "Oh, Anja, where did you hear such a thing?"

The old woman looked smug. "I heard. The facts of the matter are well known."

Jeri had to relax her face muscles consciously to stop the smile that tugged at the corners of her mouth. "The facts must not be known at all, Anja. The French yacht was struck by another boat, not some kind of demon, and no baby was eaten by a devil, because they didn't even *have* a baby. They only had a dog,

Anja, that went down with the yacht."

Anja's eyes lit up as if Jeri had proven what she said, not contradicted it. "It eats dogs, too. This is also a well-known fact."

Jeri groaned. Listening to Anja was like reading one of the back issues of the island newspaper, which she figured was significantly responsible for promoting attitudes like Anja's.

"People say your father is the smartest man they ever did see," Anja said, following Jeri to the Land Rover, "but he must precious know little yet about the raising of a girl child, the way he does give you your head. It is not the proper way, and I tell him this, you know. He should not approve of this thing you do."

"I talked it over with him, Anja. He thinks my having a look at the ruins is a good idea," Jeri said, sliding into the seat of the Land Rover.

"You are both used to the United States. You do not yet know all there is about Sabado."

"But I'm trying to find out as much as I can."

Anja pointed her finger in warning at Jeri again. "At night the devils howl and hiss from their lair . . ."

Jeri smiled through the open window and hit the starter, bringing the Land Rover to life. "Then I don't have anything to worry about, Anja. I plan to be back before night."

In the sideview mirror, Jeri saw Anja shaking her head and watching her as she drove away. The grandmotherly old lady was genuinely concerned for her, and Jeri felt bad about that, but it would have been wrong to let someone's superstitious fears prevent her from undertaking something that she hoped would be educational as well as fun.

By the time she reached the end of the drive, their house was already hidden behind the dense greenery of tropical foliage. The narrow, broken strip of asphalt that constituted the main road was steaming from a recent shower, which Jeri caught up with a few minutes later. The rain was typically Sabadoan. The island had a miniature weather system all its own, which was in constant turmoil. The drifting cell of rain pelted the Land Rover, requiring Jeri to switch the wipers to high speed, and then, within less than a mile, she was in dazzling sunshine again.

She met one of the public buses that were created by fitting bench seats on large truck beds and adding surrey tops. It was loaded with colorfully dressed people and their goats, pigs, chickens, and produce, all on the way to market at Rotole. Jeri pulled to the side to let the bus pass, and the islanders shouted and waved their greetings.

A few minutes later, she met a banana truck swaying from side to side under its heavy burden of green bananas harvested from the many small plots of the island's interior. She didn't see anyone else until she was on the dirt-and-mud cut-through to the coastal road, where an elderly man was leading a donkey cart laden with firewood that he had macheted from the forest. The trail was so narrow that the Land Rover and cart were barely able to squeeze past each other.

When Jeri broke out of the jungle onto the coast,

the sudden openness seemed shocking by comparison. The passive Caribbean lay in a flat blue haze that stretched away to meet the sky's lighter blue at the horizon. Below, the mild surf turned white against coral reefs and jagged shoreline.

Yet the road was worse here than in the interior. Chiseled out of the steep, inhospitable northwest shore, the coastal road was seldom used and in serious disrepair. It had been undercut and eroded by storms and was strewn with rocks and boulders that had dislodged from above.

Jeri shifted the Land Rover into four-wheel-drive and moved ahead cautiously. In places, the road was fifty feet or more above the rocks and surf. If the vehicle went over the edge, death was guaranteed for its driver.

It's understandable why no towns or villages had sprung up along here, Jeri thought. The sea was not easily accessible, and the combination of rocks and reefs and coral heads made the waters dangerous for boats of even moderate displacement. Yet, according to the archaeological paper she had read, these same features had made the area attractive to the civilization of transplanted Mayans. The cliffs and hazards of the water would have afforded protection from raiding parties coming from the sea and were perhaps a principal reason that the ancient civilization had been able to survive the repeated attacks of the Carib Indians long enough to leave its mark on the island.

Gradually feeling more secure with the sure-footed way the Land Rover crawled over the treacherous road,

Jeri continued up the coast. After several miles, she saw another Land Rover approaching, and as the vehicle passed in and out of view around volcanic outcrops, she soon recognized the black-and-white design of the island police car. At a wide place about a hundred yards in front of her, the car pulled to the side to give her room to pass.

"Hello, Joe," she said, stopping when their windows were only inches apart.

The handsome Sabadoan's hand went toward the brim of his hat. "A good day to you, Miss Collins."

"Jeri," she corrected. "My name is Jeri, remember?" They had met casually before, several times. Joe Matta was less than half a dozen years older than she was, and there was a kind of determination about him that she had never failed to notice. He often appeared deep in thought, as if considering several things at once.

His face broke into a pleasant smile. "Jeri," he said.

"What brings the head of Customs and police way up here all by himself?" she asked.

"What brings *me* up here?" Matta chuckled but answered. "Well, I drove this way to see if perhaps there was debris washed ashore from the French yacht."

"Did you find any?"

He shook his head. "No. But I did not really expect to. The currents would have carried it away from Sabado by now." He raised his thick eyebrows, asking the most obvious question, "What brings *you* up here?"

"I'm going to see the ruins." She held up her map

and then went into an explanation, hoping it didn't sound like tourist patter.

"Aren't you going to warn me?" she asked, when his only response was to nod thoughtfully.

He shook his head. "I am fully Sabadoan, but I do not share with many of my people a preoccupation with the supernatural." He shrugged and raised his eyebrows, smiling. "On the other hand, who am I to say what is real or unreal?"

Then he was serious again. "When I was a youngster, I went there many times, and the only sense of fear that my brave friends and I felt came from our own imaginations. But you will have more trouble getting there now than I did then. The road ends before where it is shown on your map. It has been blocked by a slide."

Jeri groaned. "I can't get around it?"

"Not by auto," Matta replied, reaching for her map and running his finger along the line that marked the coastal road. "The way is blocked approximately here," he said, "but if you do not mind a walk . . ."

"I don't mind at all."

"Then it will add but an hour or so to your journey. The road ends a few kilometers beyond the slide, and you would have to walk from there in any case." He returned the map to her. "Take care, M — Jeri. The terrain is much like the terrain elsewhere on Sabado in that it can be very rugged."

"I don't mind."

He smiled. "I can see that you don't."

"Joe, what are the ruins like?" she asked.

He shrugged. "I have not been there in several years, but they may not meet your expectations. They are not spectacular."

"They don't have to be spectacular for me. I just want to see them."

Matta nodded, again thoughtfully, and she wondered what was going on inside his head. He was an interesting man.

As she pulled away, Jeri observed him watching her in his sideview mirror, as indeed she was watching him in hers. She went more than two hundred yards before she saw him start up again.

Twenty minutes later, she reached the slide where a huge slab of rock had peeled away from the steep slope above, broken up on the way down, and covered the road with a pile of stone and earth the size of a house.

Swinging her rucksack to her shoulders, Jeri picked her way over the rubble to where the road resumed on the other side. The walking was easy and pleasant, and she came upon the largest gathering of hummingbirds she had ever seen. Hundreds of tiny, iridescent birds fed on nectar from a brilliant crop of red-and-pink tropical flowers.

Jeri reached the end of the road before she expected to. The northern tip of the island was rocky and craggy, and the terrain remained typically overgrown. The usual Sabadoan foliage flourished in the soil between the rocks, and many of the largest rock formations were blanketed by thick tangles of leafy vines. Higher up were trees: giant *gommiers* and *chataigniers*.

Looking at the sketch in the research paper she had photocopied, Jeri easily identified the coastal landmarks and began to climb the steep slope. Almost immediately she found a well-trod goat path that wound conveniently in the direction she wanted to go. A few minutes later, she reached the plateau where the ruins were supposed to be located.

Following the goat path among tree trunks festooned with vines, she saw what looked like an overgrown mound ahead, and, because of the deep shade and the mound's unimposing appearance, it took several moments for her to realize that this was what she had been looking for.

Its stones loosened by time and the ceaseless prying of tropical roots, the crumbling pyramid was little more than a scale model of the mammoth structures left by the Mayans in the Americas. A hundred feet wide at its base, it rose to a maximum height of no more than fifty feet, and it was so covered by the snaking foliage that the block-like temple at the top was nearly obscured.

There was a narrow but obvious path through the vines up the center of the wide stone steps, and Jeri started up them. All along the way, she found numerous fragments of stone that had been cast aside by looters. A few of them bore remnants of incisions and carvings.

Piles of stone rubble at each of the pyramid's four levels attested further to the centuries of looting that the site had suffered. On the narrow edge of the third level, Jeri walked around a large slab of stone that contained intricate markings abruptly interrupted by the slab's broken edge. Even to her untrained eye, it was obvious that the slab had been part of something archaeologically important. Possibly it was the base of a stela, a carved or inscribed pillar or stone often used by Mayan cultures for commemorative purposes.

At the fourth level, she experienced a feeling of height that she had not anticipated from the ground. Although not as tall as the nearby trees, the pyramid seemed a much more impressive structure from its top. For several moments, Jeri stood looking down, letting the strange sensation of where she was sweep over her.

She had turned and started for the temple's open entrance, when two nanny goats and a kid burst suddenly from the darkness inside, their hooves clattering against the rock. Jeri squeaked in surprise, then tried to calm her heart as the goats skipped warily around her and trotted down the steps.

She took a flashlight from her rucksack and sent the beam of light inside to check for any other surprises before cautiously entering herself. There were no more goats, just the smell of them in the dank interior of the temple.

Jeri played the light over the inside walls of the small cubicle. It was a sad sight. The glyphs that had been so painstakingly carved into the stone by long-ago craftsmen and artists were wrecked.

Looters had gouged and chiseled them, trying to take what had never been intended to be taken, and the results were tragic. It was painful to see the damage, and she thought how much more painful it must have been for someone who was studying to be an archaeologist to see it. In the beam of the flashlight, she compared the sketches in the research paper with what remained on the wall, and it appeared that much of the damage had been done in the twenty-five years since the paper had been written.

In fact, hardly anything was left intact. Using the research paper as a guide, she searched for depictions of the war canoe but found only pieces of it now. She spent a long time studying the broken, shattered stone, and her disappointment became a dull anger, directed in general at whoever was ultimately responsible for such plundering.

The outside walls of the temple were in much the same condition. Pushing aside vines, Jeri found more glyphs, virtually all of which had been mutilated. It made her sad; she knew the damage was not necessarily the act of hardened criminals. More than likely, it was the result of hard economic reality in the Caribbean, where the opportunity to make a small amount of money by selling an ancient piece of art was difficult to pass up. Not everyone's father was a successful engineer, she guiltily reminded herself.

She stayed at the top of the pyramid almost three hours, searching out detail, hoping to find something undamaged, but to no avail. People with eyes keener than hers had long ago combed the monument, taking or destroying everything.

On the ground again, she worked her way through

the jungle of vines around the base of the structure. At the back, she followed another goat path a short distance away from the pyramid to an automobile-sized stone slab that was mostly bare of vegetation and offered a comfortable place to enjoy a late lunch.

Sitting on top of the rock, Jeri opened the Thermos of limeade. She had been so engrossed in looking at the ruins that she had hardly noticed her thirst, but the delicious taste of the ice-cold limeade snapped it to her attention. She had to force herself to save a small amount to drink with her peanut-butter sandwich, for which she was suddenly ravenously hungry.

The food was gone in no time at all, and she was sitting comfortably, savoring a last bite of chocolate and looking out through the trees toward the sea, when something moved within her line of sight. She saw it again and thought for an instant it was the stem of a plant swaying in the breeze, but there was no breeze.

Curious, she dropped from the rock to the ground and followed a path through the trees toward the plateau's edge, until she saw the object clearly. It was the top of a sailboat's mast, rocking gently at anchorage.

Jeri walked to the edge of the cliff and, bracing one hand against a rock, leaned out cautiously to look down. Directly below her, in the flat water far inside the reef, was a trimaran, its expansive white deck in Bristol order of coiled lines and polished gear.

Near the bow, a small black dog was playing tug-of-war with an inflatable bumper, and a young man was stretched out lazily in the cockpit, reading a book. His hair had been lightened and his skin darkened by continuous exposure to the sun. Against the white of the sailboat, he was a splash of golden tan that drew Jeri's attention. It took a second look for her to realize the reason: he was entirely naked.

She was just taking this fact in, when she heard a rustling, rushing noise behind her. Reflexively, she whipped her head around.

It was already on her when she saw it. The hideous face with horns and fangs was hardly more than a blur in her vision: the thing struck her before she even had a chance to scream.

She went over the edge sideways, clawing at empty air. Five feet down, one foot glanced off a small rock outcrop, and she felt a burning sensation in her ankle as the jarring impact destroyed what remained of her balance and sent her careening, shoulders first and backward, into deeper space.

She couldn't see the water coming up at her, just her feet waving crazily against the blue sky. When she hit on her back, the surface of the sea felt like a slab of concrete.

Six

She had a diminished, vague awareness, but even when she was in the water, she felt hands tugging at her. She also knew a few moments later that she was being lifted. The shoulder in her midsection was hard and uncomfortable, and she dangled like a rag doll, unable to reach through the haze to assert herself.

When she was placed on her back, it was oddly pleasant, as if at any moment she would begin to stir from a restful sleep. Then the hands were touching her face, pulling at her eyelids. Her perceptions were beginning to clear but her return to reality was interrupted when her mouth was pried open and her nostrils pinched closed.

When she tried to exhale, she was overwhelmed with a great blast of warm air. Just before she thought she would blow up and burst like a balloon, she got a hand up and caught an ear.

"Don't do that!" she said, turning her head aside and freeing her nose. "I don't need it!"

He cupped his hand over her hand, which still held his ear, and his expression was a contortion of pain. It was the sunbather from the boat she had seen.

"I . . . I couldn't tell if you were breathing or not," he said through gritted teeth. "Would you mind? My ear?"

"Oh, sorry."

He had placed her on one of the long, cushioned seats that were on each side of the cockpit. "Are you okay?" he said.

"I guess so," she said slowly, waiting for signals from her body, "but my ankle feels . . ." She started to sit up, but he yelled, "Don't get up!"

"I'm okay. Really."

"No . . . I mean . . . I don't have any clothes on."

"Oh yeah," she replied, remembering. "I'll look the other way."

" 'Oh yeah?' " he mumbled, dropping through the companionway as soon as she turned her head. In the main cabin, he pulled on a pair of cut-offs and was topside again immediately.

Jeri had removed her shoe and was sitting up, examining her ankle. She put her foot down and flexed it, leaning on it.

"Is it okay?" he asked.

"It hurts a little, but I think it's just turned. I've

done worse," she replied, looking up at the good-looking young man, whom she judged to be about her own age.

"Sorry I wasn't dressed," he said, "but I wasn't expecting anyone to, uh, drop in."

"Did you see what happened?" she asked.

"I saw an upside-down body in the sky, but I really didn't even know it was a body until after you hit the water. I thought you were dead at first. I didn't like hauling you out the way I did — if you had had a spinal injury, I really could have done you in — but since I'm by myself, I didn't have any choice. What did you do, fall?"

"I was pushed. I was knocked over by — " She looked up the face of the cliff to the overhanging vines at the top. She saw the rock where she had been standing and the thick crowns of trees above and behind it. An icy chill went up her spine. She knew she hadn't imagined it. She couldn't have, because it had *knocked her over the cliff,* and where she was now proved it.

"By what?" he asked.

"I . . . I don't know. I was looking down at your boat, and it rushed me from behind. I barely got a glance at it, and I don't really know what I saw. But it had horns, and — "

"A goat!" he said, laughing. "I've seen several of them stick their heads out over the top. You got butted by a goat!"

She shook her head firmly. "No, it wasn't a goat. It was taller than a goat, and it had . . . there were *teeth.*"

He looked at her curiously. "Maybe something like a boar?"

"No." She shook her head again, emphatically. "It wasn't like an animal at all. At least, not like any animal I've ever seen. It was more like — I know this sounds silly, but I can't help it — it was more like some kind of monster, some *thing*!"

The first thing he had noticed about her after he laid her in the cockpit was how remarkably pretty she was. Her wet hair, plastered against her head and still streaming water, seemed only to accent her beauty. But now he looked at her a little more carefully. Maybe he had overlooked something.

"Are you sure you're all right? It was a long fall, and the way you hit . . ."

"Look," she said, narrowing her eyes, "I know you've just saved my life, but don't patronize me like that, like you think I'm crazy. I'm not."

His face relaxed, and he stuck out his hand. "Glad to meet you, Not. I go by the name of Ben Jackson myself."

The cornball humor caught her off guard. She looked disbelievingly at him, then smiled and shook his hand. "I'm Jeri Collins." He was taller and bigger-boned than he appeared at first glance, she thought; his sinewy physique, with a stomach like knotted ropes, had downplayed any obvious sense of bulk.

"Is anyone with you?" he asked. "Other than the thing that pushed you off, I mean."

"No, I'm by myself," she said, shaking her head, "but I see you have a companion." She reached out

41

and rubbed the ears of the fuzzy black dog that had been sniffing at her. The dog wagged where his tail would have been if he had had one. "What's his name?"

Ben shrugged. "I just call him Black Dog."

"Well, it's certainly fitting. He looks like he's about as black as black can get."

"I've only had him since yesterday, so his name isn't really fixed yet. I found him floating by himself, right out in the middle of the sea, about thirty miles from here." Ben shook his head in affected amazement. "It's astounding the things that float up out of the sea — and fall out of the sky."

"I bet I know where he came from!" Jeri exclaimed. "Two nights ago a yacht sank a few miles off the coast from here. The French couple who owned it made it to shore, but they lost their dog. I think you must have found him!"

Ben's face clouded, and Jeri could see that he had already become attached to the fluffy little mutt, an easy thing to do. Black Dog observed her with big, dark, adoring eyes, and she felt an immediate affection for him.

"Well, I guess they'll be glad to find out that he's still alive," Ben said without enthusiasm. "I'll return him as soon as I can."

"You can't," Jeri replied. "They left the island yesterday. By now, they're probably on their way back to France."

Ben's expression brightened. "Oh?"

"So you're probably stuck with him. I doubt that they'd come all the way back just to identify him, especially when it might not even be their dog. After all, there could be dozens of dogs floating around at sea."

"Hundreds probably," Ben said, laughing.

Jeri stood, and he took her arm, steadying her as she put her full weight on the injured ankle. She took the three steps to the other side of the cockpit.

"Well?" he asked.

"It's okay."

"Then why does it look like it's beginning to swell?"

"It hurts a little, so it may swell a little. When I say it's okay, I mean there's nothing broken, and it's not sprained, either. I've sprained an ankle before, and I know what that feels like. At the most, I've strained something. Anyway, I heal fast."

"I think it should be iced," Ben said, and before she could object, he dropped through the companionway again, returning with a plastic bag of ice that he placed on her ankle.

"That's not necessary," she insisted, but he insisted it was, so she sat down again with her leg on the seat, the ice arresting the swelling before it could get much of a start.

"How do you have ice on a sailboat?" she asked.

"There's a freezer that runs off a compressor powered by the auxiliary engine," he explained. "It's probably the only real luxury that I have. How about something dry to put on? They'll be a little big for you, but I can get you a T-shirt and pants. I used a laundry in the Virgin Islands. That's been several weeks ago, but nearly everything is still clean."

"Yeah, I bet," she replied. "You didn't look like you're very hard on clothes."

Ben managed to look only a little embarrassed. "Well, when you're at sea by yourself, there's really not any sense in wearing clothes, and I get used to being that way."

"Naked," she said.

"And my charts don't show any settlements near this end of the island, so I didn't even think about putting on clothes. I wasn't exactly expecting a skydiver. Well?"

"Well what?"

"Would you like some dry clothes?"

"No. I'm comfortable. I'll just let these dry on me." She looked up at him. "Thanks, Ben. Really thanks . . . for saving my life, I mean. It's the only one I have."

He smiled. "What were you doing up there anyway?"

"Looking at some ruins that were left by a small settlement of Mayans who came across the Caribbean from Central America a long time ago."

"Then you're a tourist," he said.

"Not exactly. I haven't been here very long, but I guess Sabado is my home for now. My father works for a company that's building a deep-water port here."

"SeaCon?"

She nodded. "Sea Construction, International."

"That's why I'm here," Ben said. "I heard SeaCon had a big project underway, and I was hoping I could get a job. Do you know if they're hiring?"

"Well, yes, they are hiring," she said, "but they're mainly just hiring islanders. Before my father came, they imported most of their workers, and it caused a lot of resentment among the Sabadoans. SeaCon's had problems here, and they're trying not to repeat their mistakes."

Ben made a face and sighed. "That's good for the Sabadoans, but not so good for me."

"There's still a chance you could get on," Jeri said encouragingly. "They'll be starting a major inventory in a couple of days; so much equipment has been stolen or lost that they don't really know what they have. They may take some outside help for that, but it would only be temporary; probably not for more than two weeks or so."

"That's exactly what I'm looking for! All I want is to work long enough to get a grub and fuel stake and be on my way again."

"Where are you going?" she asked.

"I . . . I'm not sure I really know," he said, trying not to make the statement sound as if it carried some weighty, soul-searching significance. "I just want to keep going and see things. And when I've gone far enough and seen enough, I suppose I'll know it."

"Well, where are you from?" Jeri asked, interested.

He laughed a relaxed laugh. "From a small town on the Mississippi River, a couple of hundred miles upstream from the Gulf."

"You've sailed *all the way from the Mississippi River to here*?" she said, astonished.

He nodded. "But it's taken a while."

45

"That's an incredible feat!"

Ben shrugged and said matter-of-factly, "You'd be surprised at the number of people who have sailed that distance, and considerably more."

She shook her head. "I can't imagine it. I'm impressed, to say the least!"

Black Dog, who had gradually worked his way into Jeri's lap and had been peacefully enjoying her caresses, sprang suddenly from beneath her hand. Yelping, then barking furiously, he leaped onto the deckhouse.

There was movement at the top of the cliff, and the black-and-white spotted head of a billy goat appeared and looked down at them.

"You sure that's not your monster?" Ben asked, as they watched the goat watching them.

"I'm sure," Jeri replied, and she felt the chill ripple through her again. "But I want to find out what it was that did that to me, Ben. And I left my pack on a rock near the ruins."

"I'd say you aren't in much condition to be climbing back up there and looking around, especially if it turns out you have to run from something."

"Like I said, my ankle's not that bad. I can walk on it, and if I had to, I could run on it, too." She looked at him. "If I had a little help . . ."

Ben grinned. "I don't believe in monsters."

"Neither do I."

"On the other hand, I'm not real sure I want to go chasing after something that has horns and teeth like you described, either. But the decision's been made for me already." He pointed to the yellow flag flying from the backstay. "I'm quarantined. I can't put foot ashore until after I've cleared this island's Customs."

"Oh," she said, realizing she would have to get her pack and make it back to the Land Rover by herself. "You'll have to do that at Rotole."

"I know. I arrived yesterday and was going to do it then, but I'd been at sea several days, and the tide was right to get in here, so I took advantage of the chance to grab a little rest before sailing the rest of the way to Rotole."

Jeri looked seaward. For several hundred yards out, the water was colored by reefs and coral heads. "I don't see how you got in here at all. Most boats stay out of these waters."

"That's one of the advantages to trimarans. With the displacement spread out over three hulls, they have a shallow draft. With a full load, this one draws only eighteen inches of water, so at high tide I can sail right over the top of a lot of what you see out there. A deep-keel boat wouldn't stand a chance."

"Neat," Jeri said.

"It's almost high tide now," he added, "and I've got to be pulling out of here in a few minutes. How did you get way up here? Hike?"

"Part way. I came in a Land Rover, but I had to leave it a couple of miles back because the road is blocked by a slide."

Ben reached under the cushion on the opposite seat and pulled out a chart of the island. "Show me where."

She pointed to the approximate position on the map

of Sabado's coastline, and Ben looked for a few moments, then shook his head. "I was hoping I could take you around to your car, but according to this, the reef is an unbroken barrier along there."

"Oh yeah," Jeri said in confirmation. "It's real bad. Even a trimaran couldn't get through there, I don't think."

"Too bad." He looked at her ankle again. "It looks like an awfully long way to have to hobble from here to where you left your car."

Jeri nodded. She was looking forward to it less and less.

"But if your monster shows up, you may make the distance in record time," he teased.

"Thanks," she said. "That makes me feel secure."

"Why don't you sail with me to Rotole?" he suggested. "If you can get transportation there, I'll be glad to come back with you tomorrow for your pack and car."

"I can get transportation, no problem," she replied, accepting his offer with an immediate sense of relief. After what had happened to her, she would have been apprehensive about going back alone through the dense, shadowy forest around the ruins, even without an injured ankle.

Ben broke the anchor from the bottom and hauled it aboard. As they motored out of the bay, Jeri observed the skillful way he maneuvered the broad trimaran over and around the numerous hazards of rock and coral. When he talked to her, it was without taking his eyes from the water ahead of them, and he seemed to have an uncanny ability to discern the small differences in water depth over the sharp coral formations.

When they were in deep water, Ben made use of his new passenger, giving her the helm while he ran up the sails.

"*Trike*," Jeri said, noticing the name engraved on a brass plate near the compass stand. "I like the way it sails: nice and level, no heeling at all. And so fast!"

"She's just poking along now," Ben said, although the trimaran was doing about twice the speed that a conventional sailboat would have done in the same wind. "In a stiff breeze, she'll really fly."

"Where did you get her?" Jeri asked.

Ben took two turns on the winch to sheet in the mainsail, made an adjustment to the vane steering, then sat back, satisfied with *Trike*'s trim as she knifed her way up the coastline. "A company that manufactured trimarans in Baton Rouge went bust, and I was able to get the empty hulls for a song, just like they came out of the molds. I borrowed a ski rig and towed them up the Mississippi to where I live, and then I started to work on it."

"You mean you *built* this boat yourself?"

"I had a little help from some friends, but, yeah, I did most of it by myself. It took a while, though. Almost two years."

Jeri looked at him in disbelief. "Then one day you just decided to take off? For parts unknown?"

Ben nodded thoughtfully, remembering. "It seemed more complicated at the time, but I guess that's pretty much what I did."

He went forward to close a hatch, and Jeri noticed the sure, catlike quality of his movements on deck. Even Black Dog, who darted familiarly about the boat, was no more agile. Here is one interesting guy, she thought.

When Ben returned to the cockpit and saw her sitting comfortably on the starboard seat with the wind blow-drying her hair, he found himself trying to remember the last time he had been around a girl his own age.

A month earlier on St. John, he had had dinner aboard a plush yacht with a girl and her parents. They had been served by a steward dressed in white, but that girl had been nothing like this one.

Seven

Sliding into Humpback Bay, Ben let out a low whistle. "Wow, this is really an *operation!*"

The bay was teeming with activity. Survey and dive crews were operating from work boats, and the huge arms of draglines and cranes swung and dipped above the barges and tugs that supported them. Shoreward, a pair of pile drivers hammered in ear-splitting synchrony, and big cats and heavy earth-carrying equipment, with powerful blasts from their exhaust stacks, reshaped the area of shoreline that would receive the foundation for the port's main quay.

"You can tie up over there," Jeri said, pointing to the dock behind her father's field office in the corner of the bay.

"It looks like a private dock to me," Ben said. "They

may not want me tying up there. Maybe I should just lie off and anchor."

Jeri shook her head. "Don't worry about it. It'll be okay. I promise."

Ben shrugged — she seemed to know what she was talking about — and angled *Trike* in that direction. Fifty yards out, he turned the trimaran into the wind and doused the sails, approaching the small dock under power. Fitzgerald, looking surprised to see Jeri on the boat, came from the office and caught the mooring lines that Ben tossed him, and they secured the wide trimaran to the pilings.

Jeri stepped to the dock and tested her ankle. The ice pack had checked the swelling, and it didn't feel bad at all. She knew she could have made the walk back to the Land Rover without great difficulty, but she was still glad she hadn't tried it.

"Where's my father?" she asked Fitzgerald.

"At the main office. He should be back any minute."

"He needs a Customs check," Jeri said, nodding toward Ben. "I'll see if I can get someone."

Fitzgerald returned with her to the field office, and she made a request for Customs service over the VHF radio. Joe Matta answered from the radio in his car, saying that he was nearby, and he came himself, arriving at the dock in less than five minutes.

Black Dog yapped at the stranger trespassing on his new home as Matta boarded *Trike*, but he got quiet when Ben told him to. The chief Customs officer instructed Ben to open the hatches to the outer hulls, but his inspection consisted of little more than a glance inside each. He stamped Ben's passport and welcomed him to the island.

While Ben was taking down the quarantine flag, Matta stepped back to the dock and turned to Jeri. "I was between here and the coastal road for most of the day, but I did not see your auto go by. When did you return?"

"My car is still up there, Joe. I came down the coast with him." She nodded toward *Trike*.

Matta regarded her sternly. "Are you not aware that such action is in direct violation of Customs regulations? When a boat is waiting for inspection under quarantine, at no time may another party board the boat, unless that party, too, is prepared for a Customs inspection. Technically, you have made an illegal entry, Miss Collins."

"I'm sorry," she replied, aware of the sudden and formal change in his attitude toward her. He actually sounded angry. "But I couldn't help it." She hesitated. "Well, I guess that's not true. I could have avoided sailing back with him, but it is true I couldn't avoid going aboard his boat."

"That's right," Ben said, joining them on the dock. "I made that decision. She had nothing to say about it at all."

Matta regarded them with an air that was strictly professional. "Perhaps you should explain." He said it politely, but there was no doubt that it was an order.

Jeri immediately complied, telling him the events of that morning. When she got to the part about the thing knocking her over the edge of the cliff, however, she felt suddenly foolish, and she was glad Ben was there to lend some credibility to her story.

"This animal — or what you say had horns and teeth — it charged you?" Matta asked.

"It hit me, or pushed me, or shoved me, or something. All I know is, suddenly it was there and suddenly I wasn't."

"When I saw her, she was in the air upside-down, and it sure wasn't the way somebody would jump," Ben added.

Matta looked thoughtful, giving neither of them a hint of whether he believed the story or not. Finally he looked at his watch and said, "It is too late today, but I want both of you to come to my office in the morning. We will retrieve your auto, Miss Collins, and the two of you will show me where this incident happened."

"Yessir, Mr. Matta," Jeri replied respectfully, and he nearly smiled.

"You are forgiven your neglect of the Customs regulations . . . Jeri," he said. "As for tomorrow, it is merely one of my duties to investigate such . . . such an unusual report. Since you are familiar with Sabadoan tendencies to become excited by unusual occurrences, especially in relation to anything that happens near the ruins, I hope you will exercise caution in telling anyone about this."

"We won't tell anyone but my father," Jeri said, thinking, *And especially we won't tell Anja.*

Right after Joe Matta left, a Jeep pulled into the parking area beside the building, and as soon as the driver got out, Ben knew who it had to be. As he walked toward them, it was obvious that he was curious about the trimaran moored at the dock and the young man who stood beside his daughter. To Ben, it was also obvious that the father of the girl he had pulled from the water was not merely a SeaCon hireling. He carried such a natural look of authority that he had to be someone in charge.

"Daddy!" Jeri said, filling with the kind of warmth that seeing her father always gave her, "this is Ben Jackson. Ben, this is my father, Vernon Collins, head engineer and top man of this whole operation."

"As for my being 'top man' here, she merely neglects to mention the *owners* of SeaCon," Collins said, extending his hand. "How do you do?"

"I'm pleased to meet you, sir," Ben replied.

"Ben is just passing through, but he's looking for a job," Jeri said, "one that would last about as long as it's going to take to do the inventory."

Vernon Collins was a little taken aback by his daughter's promotion of someone who was a total stranger to him, but he was more curious than anything else. He smiled. "Since you appear to be his agent, tell me — what are his qualifications?"

Jeri gave her father a curious look. "Well, for starters he fixed things so that you're still a parent."

*   *   *

The next morning Joe Matta, Jeri, and Ben reached the slide that blocked the coastal road and found the Land Rover undisturbed where Jeri had left it. Getting out of the police vehicle, Matta removed a short-barreled shotgun from the rack behind the seat and loaded it, jacking a round into the chamber. Ben and Jeri looked at each other with raised eyebrows, and Matta laughed.

"It is only a precaution," he said. "If this thing that sent you over the cliff is a maddened animal, then we may need to protect ourselves or perhaps to end the pitiful creature's misery."

Climbing over the slide, they began the walk to the ruins. It was another of Sabado's typically beautiful days, but this time Jeri felt apprehensive, as concerned that they wouldn't find anything as she was that they would.

"How's your ankle holding up?" Ben asked.

"It's fine," she said. "I think the exercise is helping it."

"Too bad," Ben replied. "I was hoping you would need to lean on me."

She looked at him and smiled.

The walk seemed longer than it had the day before, but they finally reached the end of the road, and Jeri pointed out the path she had taken to the wooded plateau. With Matta leading the way, they made the climb and walked through the trees, arriving at the base of the pyramid.

"I went up there first," Jeri said. "Then I went around back and ate lunch on a big rock, which is where I left my pack."

Matta followed the goat path around the pyramid, and Jeri and Ben followed Matta.

"It's gone!" Jeri exclaimed when they reached the big slab of stone. "It took my pack!" She felt something akin to satisfaction.

"Or something, or some person, took your pack," Matta said, examining the ground and vines around the base of the rock. "Quite possibly another person came here after you left. A few people do come up here occasionally, especially youngsters testing their courage."

"As you used to do," Jeri said.

Matta looked at her. "Yes, as I used to do." Then he asked, "What did you do next?"

"I was sitting on the rock, when I saw Ben's mast sticking up over there." She pointed through the trees toward the edge of the cliff.

"Then?" Matta asked.

"I followed the path straight out to the edge."

Walking to the edge of the cliff, they looked down into the flat, deep water. Ben pointed out where *Trike* had been at anchor, and Jeri showed Joe Matta where she had been standing.

Matta examined the ground carefully. "You had your back to the trees, and the thing that attacked you came from there?" he asked.

"I guess," she replied, and once again the feeling that she sounded foolish began to creep over her. "I . . . I heard a rushing noise, but just as I turned around, it hit me, so I guess I really couldn't tell where it came from, but it *sounded* like it came from that direction."

"And you saw that it had teeth and —"

"Yes." Jeri closed her eyes and sighed, clamping her jaws tightly. There was no way she could keep it from sounding stupid. "It had teeth and horns."

There were long moments of silence, which Ben finally filled by repeating what he had said earlier. "When I saw her, she was in the air, kind of on her back with her feet up, and she hit the water with her upper back and the back of her head."

Matta nodded. He picked a lump of dirt from the path and crumbled it between his fingers. "The impact stunned you?"

"Yes. I . . . I became aware that someone was taking me out of the water, but it was sort of confusing to me, as if it wasn't really happening."

Matta nodded again.

"But that was *after* I saw whatever it was that knocked me off from here," she added quickly. "I wasn't confused then, not when I saw it. I . . . I just didn't get a good look at it."

Matta had been squatting with the shotgun across his lap. He stood again and walked along the face of the cliff, examining the ground and grass. Then he retraced his steps, and Ben and Jeri followed him back to the pyramid.

They went up the stone steps to the temple at the top, and Matta shook his head in dismay at the broken remnants of the glyphs that had decorated the temple's walls. "I was in my teens when I was last here — not so very long ago — yet there has been much damage since even then. Now the destruction is complete."

"At one time, it must have been magnificent," Ben said. "How could anyone do this to it?"

"Greed," said Matta.

"Or merely the desire to provide for one's family, without knowing the seriousness of what they were doing," Jeri added.

Joe Matta turned and looked at her oddly, as if she had said something he hadn't expected from her. "Yes, that is also true."

Descending the pyramid, they had just reached the ground again, when a growth of vines and vegetation at one side of the path suddenly began to shake. Matta swung the shotgun to ready and simultaneously clicked off the safety. The leaves and vines shook again, and a billy goat with eight-inch horns stepped out of the foliage. The animal looked defiantly at them for a moment, then leaped sure-footedly up the side of the pyramid to the first level and disappeared around the corner.

Ben breathed a comical sigh of relief as Matta lowered the shotgun. "I thought that was it," he said. "I was prepared to be gored and eaten."

Jeri wasn't amused. "That wasn't what pushed me off the cliff. It wasn't a goat. It was as tall as a man."

"Suppose that it was a goat, and suppose that when you heard it rushing you and wheeled around, it suddenly went up on its rear legs in defense or surprise?" Matta suggested. "If it reacted in such a manner as that, then it could indeed be as tall as a man."

"No," Jeri said, but she said it too quickly and stubbornly, and it was obvious she really wasn't considering what he said. As soon as she realized that her reaction wasn't objective, she was overwhelmed with doubt. It all seemed so absurd anyway — a monster with horns and fangs. "I don't know, Joe," she said apologetically. "I really don't know what to think now. Maybe I just imagined the whole thing."

"Well, I didn't imagine seeing you fall, and I didn't imagine dragging you out of the water," Ben said in her defense.

But his words didn't help much, and all the way back to the cars, she felt gloomy and foolish. She had taken up most of Joe Matta's morning, and for no purpose at all. She found herself wishing she had never mentioned to him what had happened in the first place.

"There is a logical explanation for everything," Matta said as he was getting into his Land Rover. "But until we discover the one for this occurrence, I think it will be best that you continue to employ caution in relating the incident to others, especially with regard to the islanders."

"Don't worry," Jeri replied. "I'm not going to tell anybody. I think I'd just as soon forget the whole thing."

"We should have brought Black Dog," Ben said a few minutes later, when they were together in Jeri's car on the way back to Rotole. "He might have been able to sniff something out."

"Yeah, another goat," Jeri said morosely. "I don't think he believes me, Ben. I think Joe thinks I imagined it."

Ben shrugged. "I don't know about Matta; it's hard to tell what's going on in that man's head. But I believe you."

"Thanks," she said, meaning it. She glanced over at him from her driving and smiled. "I'm glad you're going to be around for a while, Ben. I'm glad you got the job."

"Only after you put your father on the spot like that," he said, laughing. "You didn't give him any choice but to give me the job."

"My father *always* has a choice. If he hadn't wanted to hire you, he wouldn't have." She wrinkled her nose at him. "And if you don't do good, he'll fire you, even if you did save my life."

"I'll do good, I promise," Ben said with good-humored determination that made her laugh.

They rode in silence for a while, bouncing over the rocky coastal road, and then Ben said, "I like the way you handle the car. You drive well."

"I do a lot of things well," she said.

Eight

Ben spent the final day of inventory on his hands and knees, crawling through the dust and dirt in the loft of the last of SeaCon's big steel warehouses, counting three- and five-inch pipe elbows. They had been thrown up there haphazardly — more than two thousand of them — in a space too cramped for him to stand, and he had worked all afternoon without a break to get them sorted and tabulated by quitting time.

Afterward, the spray in *Trike's* tiny shower had never felt so welcome, and since he was hooked to the dock-side water supply, he made lavish use of it. He was toweling dry, when he heard heavy footsteps on the dock. Wrapping the towel around his waist, he stuck his head through the companionway to see Brocker, the big foreman, coming toward him.

"Got your check here for you, Jackson," Brocker

said, standing at the end of the dock and waving the slip of paper.

Ben went topside and took it from him. "Thanks."

Brocker chewed on a toothpick, looking at him. "Now your job's over, you'll be pulling out of here, huh?"

"Most likely," Ben said.

"When'll that be?"

Ben shook his head. "I don't know yet. I haven't decided."

"Boat drifters," Brocker mumbled, turning away on size fourteen hobnail boots. "A breed apart."

There was something about Brocker that made Ben uneasy, but he couldn't put his finger on what it was. Brocker had had no responsibility for doing the inventory, but in the two and a half weeks it had taken to get the job done, their paths had crossed frequently, and the uneasy feeling Ben had had about him became a familiar one. Even Black Dog, who liked almost everyone, didn't wag his stub of a tail in Brocker's presence.

Ben shrugged it off and went below. One thing positive he had noticed about Brocker was that the man was competent. He definitely knew what he was doing in supervising the work crews and overseeing the use of the complex and heavy machinery involved in the construction of the port facilities. Beyond that, Ben figured anything else probably didn't matter.

He was still dressing when he heard the Land Rover turn into the parking lot at the field office. At the sound of the car, Black Dog shot up the ladder, scooted across the deck, and cleared the space between the dock and the boat without breaking stride.

Ben looked out through the deckhouse port at a now-familiar sight: Jeri, willowy and lovely in jeans and a T-shirt, absently tossing her hair behind her shoulders and walking the length of the dock toward *Trike*.

Black Dog, mad with affection, leaped, and Jeri scooped him out of the air, handling him with laughter that increased his whimpering and squirming.

"Permission to come aboard," she called out.

"Permission granted," Ben replied from inside the companionway.

Carrying Black Dog, Jeri entered the main cabin. Ben stood in front of the small mirror on the bulkhead, making a half-hearted attempt at combing order into his unruly hair.

"It's useless," he said. "It doesn't pay any attention to the comb, even when it's still damp."

She laughed and put Black Dog down, then took the comb from him. "Here, let me try."

Pursing her lips, she looked at his hair and devised a plan of attack, but it was like trying to comb a patch of briar. "The problem is you've never trained it," she said.

"True," he admitted. "All the time I was building *Trike*, I didn't care what it did so long as it stayed out of my eyes. And then after I went to sea, I just forgot about it."

"Like you forgot about wearing clothes?"

"Yeah. What you wear and how you fix your hair don't matter at sea."

"As long as you're by yourself anyway," Jeri said, putting the comb aside and using her fingers instead.

"That's right."

"There," she said, eyeing her arrangement with satisfaction. "Actually I like the way it looks: kind of unsettled." She looked into Ben's eyes and added, "Like you." They stood staring at each other for a moment, and then she glanced around. "How do you keep everything so neat? I've been in here nearly every day since you got here, and the place just gleams. You'd think there'd at least be a sock out of place."

"I don't wear socks. When you live in something this small, there's no room for clutter. Also, stuff that's not put away can get loose and become a hazard at sea, so I guess it's mainly just habit."

"Gee," she said, grinning, "the next time you need a job, maybe you could get work as a domestic. I think you would be great!"

Ben narrowed his eyes. "You're becoming a real smart act, you know that?"

"Oh?"

" 'Oh?' " he mimicked.

"Oh Ben," she said, looking at him, intently this time. "You're so serious, and then you're not serious at all. What are you really?"

"Hungry."

She laughed. "Then you're in the right condition for what we're going to do. Let's go."

"Where are you taking me this time? You've already shown me every square foot of this island."

"No," she said. "There's a village you haven't seen yet: Laudat, on the northwest shore. It's where they load bananas, and there's a neat little place there called Trina's."

* * *

Trina's was one of the island's few restaurants and, because tourism was next to nonexistent, it was little more than a part-time business for its proprietor. The four tables were outside beneath a pavilion-type roof of palm thatch, surrounded by a knee-high wall made of cement and chunks of weathered brain coral. The adjoining kitchen facilities were in a small wooden house with green sides and white shutters, and the entire area was shaded by trees.

"Do you agree?" Jeri asked, when they were seated, waiting for the dinner they had ordered.

"About what?" Ben replied.

"About this being a neat place."

He looked around as if he was considering the question, but she had already read his answer in his face. Now and then it was possible for her to tell what he was thinking, and the way that he was relaxed opposite her told her that he liked it very much, as she had known he would.

Below them was a small bay and a short wooden dock, where a stream of workers carried stems of bananas from trucks and loaded them into shallow-draft tenders. The bananas were then ferried out to a cargo ship anchored in deeper water beyond the reef. The

66

loading and unloading of the bananas was a laborious process, and it was indicative of the inefficiency that plagued the island's economy.

Ben reached out absently to pet Black Dog, who sat perched on top of the low coral wall beside them, waiting patiently for part of whatever it was that they had ordered.

"Things are going to change on this island when the deep-water port is finished," he said, shaking his head. "The banana trucks will be able to drive onto the quay beside the cargo vessels and be unloaded in a matter of minutes. That will be good, I think, but other things will change, too.

"When the tourists begin to pour in from the cruise ships, the whole island will be affected. I can imagine quaint little places like this" — he made a sweeping gesture with one arm — "turning into fast-food joints with flashing neon signs."

Jeri nodded. "I've thought about that, too. My father says it's one of life's unsolved dilemmas: the price demanded by progress. He says we have to hope for a reasonable balance between the two, so there'll still be room for a place like this. Maybe some things will be able to remain the same."

"Your father's quite a guy," Ben said.

Jeri blushed. "He likes you, too, Ben."

The young waitress brought dinner. Ben, who would try anything, had ordered the house specialty: squid cooked with vegetables in a native sauce and served with steaming plantain bananas. Jeri had ordered more conservatively, going with baked flounder and taro, a potato-like root that was a staple in the tropics. They exchanged samples from each other's plates, however, and Jeri had to admit that the squid, which she tasted only because Ben insisted and certainly not because of the way it looked, was delicious.

While they were eating, Ben noticed that the heavily loaded trucks had backed up to the dock, waiting for one of the two banana boats to return from the cargo ship. When the waitress came from the kitchen again, he pointed to a third banana boat at anchor in the bay and asked, "Why don't they use that boat, too? It would save them a lot of time."

The girl shrugged. "I think it has been sold to another man who is not in the banana business. Also, it may have troubles with the engine, you know. A time ago, some men did work on it, you know, on its mechanical parts, it seemed, but it stays where it is, without use."

"Well, that's sure not uncommon," Jeri said. "A lot of things have a way of breaking down on this island."

They finished dinner and gave Black Dog a few scraps of bread and leftovers, which he made quick work of while still sitting on top of the wall. Then they shared a glass of ginger beer, a bitter nonalcoholic drink popular among Sabadoans but which neither of them had developed a taste for. Using two straws kept them nose-to-nose, however, making the taste not so important.

"Are you glad your job is over?" Jeri asked.

"Oh, I don't know," Ben replied slowly. "The money sure was nice. I have enough to buy a radio for *Trike* now, which will be a good thing to have; I won't feel so isolated at sea, and if there's ever an emergency, I might be able to get help. Maybe I'll pick one up in Trinidad. I've heard you can find a lot of bargains there."

"Trinidad," Jeri said slowly. "That means you're thinking about leaving, doesn't it?"

Ben didn't reply, and she didn't want him to. She didn't want to hear it. She looked past him, trying not to think how empty she would feel when he did leave. On the far side of the restaurant, where the creeping tree grew over the edge of the slope, some youngsters had been playing on a tire swing. Now another boy about twelve years old joined them, and on his back was a pack.

"Ben!" she said suddenly. "I think that's my rucksack!"

Ben looked. "Are you sure?"

"I'm almost positive!"

They walked over to the kids, and it took Ben only a few minutes to work his way past the silent, shy stares into their confidence. They laughed with delight when he swung far out over the hillside in the tire swing. A few moments later he complimented the young boy on the pack and asked where he got it.

"Found it," he said without elaborating.

"Where did you find it?"

"The devils gave it to him," one of his friends said.

"What do you mean, the devils gave it to him?" Ben asked.

"What devils?" Jeri asked.

"You know, the devils," the youngster said, and he made a howling noise, while one of his friends hissed through his teeth. "The devils at the ruins of the Ancients."

Ben and Jeri looked at each other.

"They go like this," another of the kids said, and he made a high-pitched wail, causing an immediate argument to break out as to what the devils actually sounded like. Each kid had his own rendition. They ranged from wailing to crying.

"How did these devils give it to you?" Ben asked.

"Sometimes we go up the path at night to listen to them," the boy who had the pack said with a note of pride. "I went farther than they did because they were afraid, and I found it there on the path."

"Was anything in it?" Jeri asked.

"No, it was empty."

Ben looked at them with a purposefully skeptical expression on his face. "Do the devils really make noise at night, or are you just making that up?"

No, it was the truth, they said, all responding at once. The devils made their noises every night now, and anyone could hear it if they went up the path and got close enough to the ruins. The devils howled and cried and hissed, and it would make your blood run with fear, they said. They pointed at one of the younger kids, who was painfully embarrassed, and said the fear made him run all the way home to his mother.

Jeri didn't say anything about the rucksack being hers. She was only interested in where it had been found, not in having it returned.

"It's the same thing that Anja says," she said when they were in the Land Rover, driving back across the island to Rotole. "That the devils howl and hiss at night."

"We could go listen for ourselves," Ben suggested. "Although when I was up there before, I don't remember hearing anything."

Jeri looked at him. "I don't want you to think I'm superstitious, but I don't have any intention of walking up a path anywhere near those ruins at night. If I did, I might run all the way back home, too."

Ben laughed, and then he was serious. "We could sail *Trike* up there and listen from near where I was anchored before. We could even put the outboard on the dinghy and motor around to Trina's and have some more of that squid, if we wanted to. That was really good stuff!" He glanced aside from driving to look at her. "Thanks for taking me."

"You're welcome," she said.

Nine

The sea was white-capped and the sun brilliant against it. *Trike* reached, flattening the sharp chop beneath the bows of her three hulls. The trimaran moved like a speeding car over a gravel road, bumping but sure-footed, her ride level and pleasant for the two people drinking iced tea in the spacious cockpit.

The brisk wind held steady, and the vane steering maintained the heading along the jagged coastline so well that Ben did not touch the helm until they were past the point of the island. Then, turning downwind, he dropped the jib and approached the treacherous coral with the mainsail out to starboard.

Closer in, they furled the remaining sail in favor of the diesel. Clinging to the forestay at the bow, Ben shielded his eyes against the glare and concentrated on spotting the mushrooming coral heads. Jeri's palms were sweaty on the wheel, and when he motioned one way or the other, she threw the helm over in a hurry.

"Quickest reactions I ever saw," he said as they glided safely into the flat glassy water of their anchorage.

"It made me nervous," she confessed.

"It has the same effect on me, but it wasn't as bad this time because there were two of us. When I'm by myself, sometimes I have to swallow to keep my heart down."

Jeri pointed to Black Dog, who eyed them lazily from where he lay curled up in a corner of the seat. "It doesn't seem to have bothered him very much."

"I'm beginning to think nothing bothers Black Dog," Ben laughed.

They dropped the anchor into a patch of sand, and Ben backed down, making the anchor dig in securely. They were much farther out than where Ben had anchored on the day he had first come to the island.

"If a devil is going to get one of us, he'll have to swim a ways to do it," he said laughingly.

"Yeah, that's just great," Jeri replied with considerably less humor. "Already I'm beginning to feel like a piece of bait."

"Don't tell me you're beginning to believe all this stuff about devils."

"The only thing I believe is that something pushed me off that cliff," she said.

Ben nodded thoughtfully and looked toward the

shore. "But I was here all night long, and I didn't hear anything."

"Maybe you weren't listening," she said.

"That's a possibility," he admitted. "I don't sleep at sea very well. I just catnap. When I got here, I was dead tired and went out like a light."

"Well, I doubt that I'm going to sleep at all tonight."

Ben looked at her. "We could play cards — or something."

Jeri smiled.

"What about supper?" he asked. "We can take the dinghy inside the reef to Trina's, but it's three or four miles and we wouldn't make it back until after dark."

"What's the alternative?"

Ben pointed over the side. "I think we can do pretty well right here."

Jeri changed into her swimsuit, and Ben stripped to cut-offs. In snorkel gear, they stepped from *Trike*'s stern and plunged flat-footed into the sea. They surfaced amid a froth of bubbles and kicked face down, over an underwater world of spectacular beauty.

The water was so clear that the sensation was like flying. Thirty feet up, they soared above a landscape brilliant with color. Turning, they looked back at *Trike*, whose three hulls hung motionless, as if suspended in air.

Jeri dived, and Ben watched as she kicked downward, parting a school of flashing silver fish and streaming bubbles above the rust and purple of staghorn and fan coral. Propelled by flippered feet and slender legs, she glided effortlessly, and the sight of the fluid movement of her body put a hard knot in Ben's stomach.

She surfaced, intoxicated with what she had seen. "I can't believe it!" she exclaimed. "All the time I've been on this island and this is the first time I've been snorkeling here! I've dived and snorkled in a lot of places, but this is *truly* incredible! How could I have overlooked it?"

"You just didn't have me around to show you the things that count in life," he said, grinning.

Her eyes narrowed in humor behind the glass of her face mask, and she splashed him in response to his mock conceit, then dived again. Carrying his spear gun in a gloved hand, Ben followed her down this time, and they kicked side by side through a wonderland of coral.

Unperturbed by their presence, the fish had evidently seen few divers. Snapper and grouper were abundant, presenting easy targets, but several sets of antennae sticking out from pockets in the coral made Ben realize he wouldn't need to use the speargun. Prodding with the tip of the spear, he worked a large spiny lobster from its cover and pinned it quickly with his gloved hand.

When he triumphantly withdrew the crustacean from the cloud of silt, Jeri clinched her hands and nodded in approval. Returning to *Trike,* Ben tossed the lobster over the stern into the cockpit. Black Dog scrambled outside the coaming and stared down warily at the thing crawling over the cockpit floor from a safer distance.

"One more should do it," Ben said.

He missed the next lobster and had to come to the surface. He hyperventilated and dived again. He got the one after that, and both lobsters went into a boiling pot of sea water in *Trike*'s galley.

While Jeri showered and changed clothes, Ben set the small dinette and made a salad with watercress they had picked up at the market in Rotole. He lit a candle at the center of the table and served the steaming lobster with melted butter and lime juice.

"And Texas toast made with Sabadoan bread," he said, adding the grilled and buttered toast to the spread as Jeri slid into the bench seat on one side of the dinette.

"Wow," she said softly, looking in wonder at what he had put in front of her. "It looks sumptuous."

"Sorry I don't have any fine china. The metal plates are purely functional; they don't break. I also happen to be fresh out of wine," he joked. "However, we still have about a gallon of tea."

"White or red?"

"Sort of in between," he said, filling her glass.

Jeri pushed her wet hair behind her and sampled the fare. "Oh, Ben, this is *so good!*"

"You're hungry," he said modestly.

"No, really, it's delicious!" She looked over the flame of the candle at him and smiled a teasing smile. "For your next job, maybe you *could* find work as a domes-

76

tic. I think you would look especially pretty in an apron."

Ben pointed his fork at her. "Your smart mouth is still going to get you in trouble."

Her smile widened with pleasure. "You sound just like my father. He says the same thing sometimes, and he doesn't mean it, either."

Ben groaned. He had seen the way she handled her father — with ease. And she didn't try to bend her father to her will. She just did it by being herself.

"You don't like my mouth?" She pulled her lower lip out and tried to look down at it. She felt goofy with pleasure. "I've always thought it was an okay mouth. Maybe not the best mouth in the world, but at least okay." She looked up at him. "I like your mouth, Ben. And your eyes. I especially like your eyes. And your nose. I like your nose, too. In fact, I like your whole face."

Ben was looking at her mouth. It was dusk outside, and her lips looked moist in the glow of the candle light. He leaned across the narrow dinette, over the lobster and the candle. There was no doubt that he was going to kiss her — until he began to smell his T-shirt scorching above the candle flame. He jerked upright and barely managed to beat the flame out before his chest caught fire.

Jeri laughed, and then Black Dog yapped, demanding something from the table. She broke off a crust of toast, dipped it in lime-butter and gave it to him.

The lobster and salad were enough to satisfy their hunger without making them feel stuffed, and after

77

dinner they washed the few dishes together. It was a tight fit for two in the tiny galley, but they didn't mind. The closeness made talking easy.

"What are your parents like?" Jeri asked.

Ben shook his head. "My mother died when I was a baby, and my father was a marine in Vietnam. There was a mine called a Bouncing Betty, and one day he stepped on one. It killed him."

"Oh," she said softly, "I'm sorry."

"Well, I don't remember my mother at all, and I was so young when my father was killed that I can only barely remember him."

"How did you grow up? Who took care of you?"

"I have an uncle — my father's brother — and I lived with him, or in his house anyway, in the town where I built *Trike*. He's an okay guy, but he's an accountant with a big corporation that owns a lot of other corporations, and his job is to audit all these companies, so he travels all over the country. At the most, I would only see him a couple of weekends each month, so I guess I sort of grew up on my own."

Jeri nodded. "I guess that's why you seem so independent."

Ben shrugged. "I don't know about that."

"You're one of the most independent people I've ever met."

He shrugged again and seemed a little embarrassed by the observation.

"So you grew up in this Mississippi River town you mentioned?"

"Fredricksburg," he said. "It's just a little place, where my uncle happened to own a house."

"And one day you started building *Trike*."

Ben smiled at her. It was difficult to sum up what building *Trike* had been like, the way he had become obsessed with the project and what it had come to mean to him.

"I got interested in sailboats when I was in junior high school, when my uncle gave me a little Sunfish that I used to sail on the river. Then the summer before my senior year in high school, I heard about a boat company in Baton Rouge that was going out of business. The hulls were just fiberglass shells. They were offered so cheaply I couldn't pass them up.

"I gave up football, basketball, track. I gave up dates. I gave up every spare minute I had my senior year to work on her." He looked around the trimaran's finely crafted interior as if he might have had doubts that it had been worth the sacrifice. "I worked sixteen-hour days on her the summer after I graduated. I sold my bicycle, I sold my guitar and my cornet, I sold my stereo, I sold my television set, and finally I even sold my car to buy materials. I enrolled in a local junior college last fall, but I dropped out at the end of one semester because it was keeping me from working on her. I had her almost finished by then. A month later she was finished, and I launched her."

"Into the Mississippi?"

"Into the Mississippi."

"And here you are."

79

"And here I am."

Jeri shook her head and looked at him in amazement. "That's incredible, Ben. How could you have done all that?"

"One day at a time," he replied.

"That's the way it still is for you, isn't it? You exist one day at a time."

He shrugged and smiled. "I guess."

Jeri looked up at him. She put her arms around his neck, and then suddenly they both froze. A high, shrill scream pierced the night air like a jolt of electricity. Moments later the scream was followed by a dying howl that seemed to float without direction from the darkness around them.

Black Dog's ears went up and the hair stiffened on his spine. Barking, he leaped from the cushion of the dinette seat and shot up the ladder into the cockpit.

Ten

Growling and snarling, paws thumping and pattering on the deck, Black Dog raced from one side of *Trike* to the other. Finally, Ben ordered him quiet. Jeri scooped the small dog up and held him, quivering and whimpering in her arms.

"What on earth was that?" she asked nervously.

Ben shook his head, though in the dark she could barely see him. "I don't know."

It came again — the same shrill scream, followed by a chilling, moaning howl that intensified two more times before dying completely. After a few seconds of silence, a new noise, a long hissing sound, rushed out over the water toward them and made the hair on Jeri's neck stand up. Black Dog stiffened.

"Oh Ben," Jeri said in a hushed voice, "I don't like that *at all!*"

"I just hope that whatever it is doesn't know how to swim!" he replied.

"That's not funny, Ben."

"I'm not trying to be funny. I'm serious! Listen," he said, but was interrupted by still another scream. When it ended, he said, "There's another noise."

"It sounds like somebody being tortured."

"No, not that. There's something else."

Ben held up his hand, and they listened intently. "There," he said quietly, "do you hear that?"

She shook her head. "I'm not sure . . ."

"Thunka-thunka-thunka," he said, moving his hand in rhythm.

The sound was so faint that Jeri wasn't sure it was a noise at all. It was more of a feeling, a steady pulsing that she could have easily confused with the beating of her own heart. So subtle was it, they weren't sure when it stopped. Ben continued moving his hand, until he realized there were no longer any pulses to move in time with.

"What was — " Another long, drawn-out hiss interrupted Jeri, and another chill moved in a wave from the base of her spine to the back of her head. Black Dog growled, and Jeri squeezed him tightly, more for her own comfort than his.

Ben shook his head. "Man, that is *weird*!"

"I don't like it, Ben," Jeri said again. "I really don't. It's eerie!"

"I thought you weren't superstitious," he said.

"I'm not, but I'm giving serious consideration to changing my mind. It's just like Anja said: devils moaning and howling and hissing. At least that's what it sounds like!"

"There's a logical explanation for everything," Ben said.

"Keep telling me that."

The moon was low on the horizon, and they could barely make out the dark ragged crown of trees at the high point of the island. It was almost impossible to get a bearing on the sounds, but when the next scream sliced through the night air, it seemed to come from the direction of the ruins. Jeri imagined it curling from the opening of the temple at the top of the pyramid, and she shuddered. The ravaged temple had seemed only that — ravaged — when she had been inside it. Now its image turned sinister in her mind.

"Ben, what's that at the base of the cliff?"

"What's what?"

"It looks like light," she said. "See how you can almost make out the rocks, like there's light reflecting off the water? Only there isn't any light to reflect off the water, except maybe for the moon, and the moon's in the wrong place to do that."

They were more than a hundred fifty yards offshore, and it took Ben a moment to discern what Jeri was talking about. But once he saw it, it became increasingly apparent: a faint glow at the waterline that cast a barely detectable illumination against the base of the cliff.

The moon was in the wrong position and the stars were not bright enough to be responsible for the light. And the noises — there was simply nothing that could explain them. Finally, Ben took a flashlight and untied the inflatable dinghy from the foredeck.

"What are you doing?" Jeri asked, afraid she knew full well what he was doing, but hoping she was wrong.

"Going over there."

"Ben, let's think about this first."

"What's there to think about? It's what we came up here for, isn't it? We wanted to find out if we could hear what those kids said they heard. Well, we can. And we can see something, too, but we're not going to find out what any of it is way out here."

"So maybe we should just quit while we're ahead, huh?"

Ben picked up the inflatable and dropped it over the side. "You know you don't mean that." He pulled the dinghy around to the boarding ladder. "Let's go."

"*Let's* go?"

"You don't think I'm going over there by myself, do you?"

Jeri groaned in dismay.

Ben pointed the beam of the flashlight down into the dinghy. "Get in."

Jeri groaned again, in resignation this time. "What about Black Dog?"

"Leave him here. He can ward off any boogiemen that try to get aboard."

Black Dog, who would usually wait patiently aboard *Trike*, didn't like being left behind this time. As they rowed away, he whined and whimpered plaintively and would have gone overboard after them had Ben not given him a stern "No!" just as the little dog was gathering to jump.

"Lucky Black Dog," Jeri said, and then another of the chilling howls came from the island, and through her teeth she added, "poor us!"

"Keep the light out," Ben said. "No sense in announcing our arrival."

The water inside the reef was flat and dark. Ben drew the oars silently. Closer in, the light was more visible, faintly illuminating a large area of the water. They hadn't heard any more of the noises since they had gotten into the dinghy, and Jeri was beginning to think that maybe they had stopped. That thought was interrupted by another long, drawn-out hiss that seemed to come right out of the face of the cliff toward them. Jeri went rigid, and Ben stopped the oars in mid stroke.

"Don't you think we're close enough?" Jeri asked softly.

Ben resumed pulling the oars. "The light's coming from the water!" he said, twisting his neck to look over his shoulder.

Suddenly Jeri was aware that she could see the blades of the oars, dark underwater silhouettes that were back lit. The dinghy glided in close to the cliff, and Ben turned the dinghy slowly.

They floated on a sea of soft light. It came up around them, illuminating their throats and casting shadows up their faces.

"Ben, I'm not liking this!"

He leaned his head out over the side of the dinghy and looked down. The light on his face gave him a ghostly appearance. "It's coming from out of the rocks of the cliff, down near the bottom. Look!" he said.

The first thing Jeri noticed was a large school of fish swimming through the shaft of light that seemed to scatter upward through the clear water from the very base of the cliff. The spray of light was indirect but powerful enough to draw a crowd of sea life.

"It's deep," Ben said. "At least fifty or sixty feet down."

"What do you think it is?" Jeri asked.

"I don't have any idea. I've never seen anything like it."

"It's creepy, Ben."

"Yeah, I'll go along with that."

"I think where we ought to go is away from here."

Ben continued to look, trying to determine the cause of the light, but the water was too deep and there were too many fish in the way. Then, suddenly, the light went out, and they were once more floating on black water.

"Well, that does it for me," Jeri announced flatly. "I've had enough. It's been real interesting and everything, but I want to go back to the boat now." When he didn't reply, she switched the flashlight on. He was still looking into the water, and the light in his face nearly blinded him.

"Do you mind?" he asked, waving his hands to fend off the light.

"Listen, Ben, if you're not going to use the oars,

give them to me, okay? I want to get out of here."

"Don't you want to go ashore?"

"Are you out of your mind? *No*, I don't want to go ashore. What's more, I'm *not* going ashore. Now row!"

"You couldn't pay me to go ashore in this dark right now, either," Ben confessed, and he began to row.

"Then row a little faster if you don't mind."

As their eyes adjusted to the darkness again, they were able to see each other without using the flashlight and could even make out the vague shape of *Trike*.

"The noises have stopped, too," Ben observed, drawing them nearer the trimaran.

"I've noticed," Jeri replied. "Do we have to stay here tonight, Ben? Couldn't we sail down to Laudat and anchor there?"

"I'd rather not risk trying to make it through the coral in the dark. It's hard enough to get through when we can see. Besides, if anything was going to get us, it probably would have already done it by now. I think we'll be safe enough."

"I hope you're right," she mumbled. "I know I'll feel better when we get out of this dinghy."

They were about thirty yards from *Trike* when they heard Black Dog. Jeri cast the light toward the trimaran, and they saw him standing at the stern, leaning out beneath the lifeline, whining and whimpering. Then he began snarling and barking furiously.

Feet stiff and dancing, he jumped from side to side, his lips curled and small sharp teeth bared, barking savagely.

87

"What's the matter with him?" Jeri asked.

"I don't know," Ben answered, puzzled. "Black Dog! Hush, you mutt! It's just us!"

But Black Dog didn't hush. He became even more animated, snarling viciously and throwing specks of saliva from his mouth as if he had gone mad.

Jeri held the light on him, and then swung the beam. Her voice trembled. "Ben, I think it's something else."

The water stirred to one side of the dinghy, and she whipped the flashlight around.

She saw it clearly this time — the curl of horns, the curve and point of fangs and the hideous face. Dripping and slimy, it came up from the black depths. Its horrid claw hooked over the side of the dinghy and reached for her.

Jeri recoiled, screaming. The flashlight flew from her hand as Ben snatched an oar up and speared into the dark. The dinghy upended, and they spilled out into the sea.

Jeri fought for the surface, but something closed tightly on her ankle, pulling her down.

She kicked wildly. As suddenly as she had been seized, she broke free and shot, gasping, to the surface.

"Ben! Oh god, Ben!"

"Swim to the boat! Hurry!"

Jeri made the boarding ladder and flew onto the deck. She looked back and saw Ben reaching for the overturned dinghy. Spinning, wary, he treaded high in the water.

"Where is it?" he shouted.

88

"I don't know! I don't see it!"

Ben caught the dinghy's bow line and snatched the light craft around.

"Oh Ben, it was underneath! It *had* me! Get out of there! *Get out of there!*"

Ben put the line to the dinghy between his teeth and swam quickly. Coming up the ladder, he dropped the dinghy's line over a cleat, then looked out over the stern. But there was nothing — only water and darkness.

"Whatever it was, it's gone," he said.

Jeri clung to him, digging her fingers into his arm. "Did you see it?"

"I saw it."

"It followed us out here. What was it? *Oh lord, what was it?*"

"I don't know."

* * *

Ben got his speargun and loaded it, pulling both rubbers back. They stayed in the cockpit all night without sleeping. Except for an occasional fish, however, nothing stirred in the water around them, and Black Dog was quiet.

At dawn they made the short run to Laudat, dropped anchor among the banana boats, then caught the public transport back to Rotole.

Eleven

Vernon Collins leaned back in his chair behind his desk at SeaCon's main headquarters high on the hill above Humpback Bay and shook his head at the improbable tale that he had just heard.

"Strange screams, a light at the bottom of the sea, and a monster," he mused. "You two haven't been eating fermented coconuts, have you?"

"Oh, Daddy," Jeri groaned, "it happened just like we said!"

"How big was this, ah, monster?" he asked.

"We didn't see all of him," Ben replied. "But his head was about the size of a man's, maybe a little bigger."

"And it couldn't have been a sea creature, say a porpoise or some other animal that was disfigured?" he asked.

Jeri shook her head emphatically. "No, Daddy, it wasn't anything like that."

"It wasn't like anything I've ever seen," Ben said, agreeing.

Collins nodded, thinking, then reached for his phone. "I'll have one of the staff get Joe Matta on the radio —"

"No," Jeri said quickly. "The last time I got him to go up there, I felt like a fool, and I don't want to go through that again."

Her father shrugged. "Then what do you propose to do?"

Jeri and Ben exchanged glances. "We want you to let us borrow some of SeaCon's scuba gear," she said.

Collins looked at them in modest disbelief. "From the way you two described what happened, I would think that would be the last thing you wanted."

"We want to find out what's going on up there," Jeri said.

"We thought we'd try to locate where the light was coming from," Ben said.

"But not at night," Jeri said. "We'll dive in the daytime, when it's safe."

"When we *think* it's safe," Ben corrected. "We don't really know if it's risky or not, but it seems to me that if that thing was serious about getting us, it could have done it when we were in the water. It didn't."

"Or at least it didn't succeed," Collins said. "But suppose next time it does?"

Jeri made a face of concern, but Collins noted the determined look that meant his daughter had already made up her mind. He sighed. "Okay, I'll see that you get the gear, provided that you put off your dive until tomorrow."

"Why?" Jeri asked.

"Because I need you today. Both of you." There was a large manila envelope on one side of his desk. Opening it, he withdrew a long computer print-out. "Accounting has finished running the inventory, and this is the listing of missing equipment." Collins shook his head in dismay. "It's incredible, absolutely incredible. I was told there had been a lot of stealing going on before we came here, but I had no idea it was so extensive. There are literally thousands of items missing, and not all of it little stuff, either."

He pointed with his pencil, making check marks as he went down the computer list. "Among other things, this company has lost four ten-kilowatt generators, two portable compressors, more than fifty heavy-duty lead-acid storage batteries, several electric motors, enough tools to outfit an automotive plant, and an assortment of very expensive pieces of cutting and grinding equipment, including some of the finest industrial quality diamond-edged blades available.

"The only thing I can figure is that there must have been some kind of organized theft ring in operation before we stopped their activities by increasing security. Some of these items, such as the generators and batteries, would be handy things to own on an island like Sabado, but the generators would be especially difficult to conceal."

"They'd be a cinch to dispose of elsewhere for cash

though," Ben said. "Once you got them off the island, you could sell them anywhere from Trinidad to the Virgins. Electricity on most of the islands is unreliable at best, so they'd be snapped up at almost any price, no questions asked."

Collins nodded. "That's what I'm thinking, too, Ben."

"But what's that got to do with Ben and me?" Jeri asked.

"SeaCon has a lawyer on retainer in Pointe-à-Pitre, Guadeloupe." Collins pulled a business card from a desk drawer and attached it to the print-out with a paper clip. "Here's his address. A Mr. Henri Morgeaux. SeaCon says Morgeaux will be responsible for notifying the various Caribbean authorities to be on the alert for any of our equipment. I want you to get this list to him today, Jeri, and I'd like you to go with her, Ben, because you're familiar enough with the equipment to answer any questions Morgeaux might have. SeaCon will pay your expenses, plus a full day's wages, if you'll accompany her." He narrowed his eyes and looked at him in a way that made Ben suddenly uneasy. "In other words, you'll be getting paid for what you've been doing for free lately."

"Yessir," Ben replied, feeling his face flush. "I'll be glad to go with her."

Jeri smiled and got up from her chair. Leaning across his desk, she kissed her father on the cheek and picked up the print-out.

"Let's go, Ben."

"In case I'm out of the office when you get back, I'll

93

leave word with the diving chief to let you have the scuba gear, but promise me you'll be careful."

"Thanks, Daddy," she said. "We will be."

"One other thing," he said, stopping them as they were going out the door. "Are you going to be staying out all night again?"

Ben felt his ears turn red. He looked down at his shoes and studied the way he had tied the laces.

"Well," Jeri replied slowly, as if giving the question deep consideration, "if I stay on Ben's boat tonight, we'll be able to get started on our dive first thing in the morning and save all that time it takes to drive across the island."

"Which is a whole twenty-five minutes," Collins said.

"Well, Daddy, every minute in life counts, you know."

Her father rolled his eyes and shook his head as if he had heard more than he wanted to. "Then you tell Anja. She gave me the devil this morning. She said I wasn't a fit parent."

Jeri walked back across the office and unabashedly hugged her father's shoulders from behind, lovingly putting her head in the crook of his neck.

"We both know that's not true, don't we, Daddy?"

Twelve

Twin engines roaring, the Leeward Island Air Charter seaplane gained speed rapidly across the chop of Humpback Bay. The water grew hard beneath its pontoons, and with a practiced hand the pilot eased back on the yoke, separating the aircraft from the sea and turning it skyward.

"Now this is what I call traveling in style," Ben said, his forehead pressed against the window as he watched the coral formations slip by beneath them. "An entire airplane, just for the two of us!"

"First class all the way," Jeri replied from beside him, "compliments of SeaCon International."

When they had gained a few hundred feet of altitude, the pilot put the plane in a shallow bank and Humpback Bay turned slowly off the axis of one wing, the huge cranes, barges, and construction equipment shrinking to the size of toys as the aircraft continued to climb.

The plane skirted the shore of the island at five hundred feet, revealing an aerial view of Sabado's incredibly rugged terrain, the peaks of which rose several times higher than they were flying. The jungle of the island's lush interior, broken only by the windings of numerous rivers, resembled an undulating green carpet.

"Look!" Jeri said, pointing. *"Trike!"*

There was no mistaking the trimaran. Inside the reef at Laudat, its broad deck was a brilliant splash of white among the dull-colored banana boats anchored around it. And on the cockpit seat was a contrasting spot the color of India ink.

"Black Dog!" Ben said, laughing.

The plane banked away from the island and resumed climbing. Rising from the blue sea in the distance ahead of them was a hazy purple cone, a tropical island that was formed by the peak of an underwater mountain.

"That's Marie Galante," Jeri said, "and on the other side is Guadeloupe. We'll just fly straight to it."

In minutes, Guadeloupe appeared like a ghost out of the haze, stretching out on both sides of Marie Galante, its own peaks reaching up to surpass the height of its smaller sister; and less than an hour later, the pilot began shedding altitude, descending into Petit Cul de Sac Marin, a large bay at the center of the island. Below them, the sea was specked by fishing boats, trawlers, container ships, power yachts, and sailboats, trailing white wakes over the blue and blue-green water.

"This is amazing," Ben said. "If we had come by boat, we'd barely have the anchor up by now. It can take *days* to go this far by wind power."

Jeri gave him a knowing smile. "But in an airplane like this, all we can do is sit. In a sailboat like *Trike*, there are other things we could do to pass the time, which is in keeping with your philosophy. It may not be so much where you go in life, but more a matter of how you get there. I'm thinking we could have a lot more fun getting here if we had come on *Trike*."

"Yeah," Ben agreed, "but I'm also enjoying this."

The pilot reached the tower at the Pointe-à-Pitre airport by radio and received clearance to put down in the bay. They dropped in quickly, the seaplane's pontoons settling smoothly onto the surface of the water. At the Customs dock, a pair of muscular men in T-shirts secured the craft to its berth, swung out a gangplank, and opened the door for the two passengers.

A white-gloved official waited to take their passports and asked in French how long they intended to be in Guadeloupe.

"Ce jour. C'est tout," Jeri replied.

"You speak French," Ben said, surprised.

"Only a little," she replied, but she spoke enough of it to respond to the rest of the official's questions and thank him after he had stamped and returned their passports. Moreover, when they hailed a cab in front of the Customs Office, she used French to tell the driver where they wanted to go.

"I'm impressed," Ben said, when they were sitting together in the cramped back seat of the small taxi.

"Good. I want you to be. But it's only high school fluency, and barely that." She leaned against him. "Look at this place, Ben. It's everything Sabado isn't."

Pointe-à-Pitre was noisy and crowded and, for a Caribbean city, thoroughly modern. The four-lane highway into the city was jammed with traffic, and most of the drivers seemed to keep one hand on the horn. High-rise apartment and office buildings were a dramatic contrast to the basic, subsistence-level structures of backward Sabado, and billboards advertising the products of French and multinational corporations attested to the island's lively economy. There was beauty in the green peaks and valleys of the outlying countryside, but Pointe-à-Pitre's main message was one of commerce, French commerce.

"I'm glad Sabado isn't like this," Ben said with a note of distaste. "And I hope it never is."

Jeri laughed. It seemed absurd. "I don't see how it could be."

"A deep-water port might do it."

She shook her head. "Sabado has too much of its own flavor. No foreign economic power could ever influence it to the degree that the French have influenced Guadeloupe. The port should only bring necessities. This is excessive. I can't imagine Sabado becoming like this."

"I hope you're right."

* * *

They took the elevator to the fourth floor of a down-

98

town steel-and-glass high-rise and entered the thickly carpeted reception room to a suite of offices. In French, Jeri told the receptionist that they needed to see Henri Morgeaux, and after she had explained with difficulty that they were from SeaCon *"avec les papiers de l'inventaire,"* the attractive woman smiled and answered in perfect English.

"Yes, Mr. Morgeaux has been advised to expect a report. He is presently with a client but should be able to see you within half an hour, if you care to wait."

They waited forty-five minutes, and then the receptionist ushered them down a short hallway and through the large doors of a private office. Morgeaux rose from behind his desk and greeted them warmly. He was tall and dark-haired, and although his looks and dress were unmistakably French, he, too, spoke impeccable English.

"Please be seated," he said, indicating the chairs opposite the desk. "I believe you have the listing of missing items from the inventory of SeaCon's project at Sabado, is that correct?"

"Yes," Ben replied. "Jeri?"

She had the computer print-out on her lap, but she had heard only vaguely anything said beyond the initial introductions. Instead, she was gazing in stunned amazement around the lavish, spacious office, which was decorated with a dozen of what looked like priceless pieces of Mayan art.

"Jeri?" Ben repeated. "The print-out."

"Oh, I'm sorry," she replied, placing the folds of

paper on the desk. "I was just admiring your office, Mr. Morgeaux. The artwork — it's Mayan, isn't it?"

"Yes, indeed," he said, his voice reflecting his pride in his possessions. "A small collection but a large passion. Are you a connoisseur of such things, Miss Collins?"

Jeri shook her head. "No, not at all. But I do have an interest. Would you mind if I looked? Ben's the expert on the inventory anyway. He can tell you everything you need to know."

"Of course," Morgeaux said graciously. "Please make yourself at home."

While Ben and the attorney put their heads together over the print-out, Jeri made her way around the office. The art objects were varied. There were several stone figures of gods or gods-and-serpents that looked as if they had been chiseled and removed from larger pieces of stone. There was an excellent example of a stone calendar, largely intact, and behind a sheet of glass on the wall was a section of codex, an intricate painting of Mayan figures that an ancient craftsman had delicately scribed on paper.

An exquisite Mayan vase occupied a position on its own pedestal in one corner of the office and was obviously a main showpiece. On it was the figure of a woman with jade inlays in her teeth and a male dancer wearing a jaguar-skin headdress and pants, with a snake above his head.

But what attracted Jeri's attention most of all was the huge glyph on the wall behind Morgeaux's desk. Of darker stone than the other objects, it was at least four-by-eight feet and was mounted in a single piece on a heavy wooden frame. She returned to her seat to get a closer look just as Ben was finishing explaining how to read the summary codes at the end of the print-out.

"It is truly an immense amount of material that is missing," the attorney said, shaking his head, while Jeri looked above him, her eyes following the intricate carvings in the glyph's separated blocks. "I had no idea thievery had been so rampant. I will of course send copies of this to the various authorities through-out the Caribbean, as the executives at SeaCon wish. However, it is my guess that very little of it, if any at all, will be recovered."

Ben nodded his agreement. "But it's at least worth a try. Some of this is expensive stuff."

The SeaCon business at an end, Jeri gestured with one hand around them and asked, "Where did you get all these . . . these beautiful things?"

Morgeaux's smile was tolerant. "A collector does not reveal his sources. Suffice it to say, however, that I gathered them in many ways and over many years. Do you like them?"

"Oh yes. They're lovely," Jeri replied. "Of course, I know very little about Mayan art, but I was under the impression that the countries where it's found are go-ing to great pains to restrict its removal."

"True," Morgeaux said, "but most of these items have been in circulation for many years. If I did not have them, someone else would. There is great de-mand, and when people are willing to pay the price, whatever the price may be, it is impossible to stop the trade."

Right, Jeri thought, suddenly beginning to develop a distaste for the man. As long as there were wealthy French attorneys willing to shell out the money, that was probably a certainty. Great and irreplaceable works of ancient art would continue to be lost forever. She looked up at the big glyph again, her eyes moving from block to block.

"All of this came from Central America?" Ben asked.

"Yes, of course," Morgeaux replied, and a trace of impatient annoyance had invaded his voice, as if he considered the question founded in ignorance. "The Maya *were* the Americas."

"There are remains of a small culture on Sabado," Ben replied.

Morgeaux looked indignant, and a moment later, he shrugged, scoffing. "A splinter group perhaps but hardly more than a small family when compared to the great Mayan civilization of the Americas.

"Besides," Morgeaux continued, "its small treasures were wiped out years ago. A tragedy, of course."

Yeah, Jeri thought, a tragedy caused by people willing to pay, whatever the price.

The stone carvings of the glyph were complex and the curving overlap of lines, as well as the unusual figures of men and animals, sometimes in combination, played tricks with her perceptions. For an instant she thought that what she saw was a product of her imagination confusing the shapes, and then she began to make it out plainly. It was in the very center of the next-to-last block on the glyph, and there was no mistaking it at all.

When Jeri looked at Ben to let him know that she was ready to go, she was poker-faced, but because he was beginning to know her so well, he also saw that she was suddenly very excited.

Thirteen

From a table at Trina's, they watched the sun go down. It slipped red and glorious into the sea, far out beyond where *Trike* sat at anchor among the banana boats inside the reef, and the night came a few minutes later while they were still eating. The young girl who waited on them lit the lanterns that hung from the edge of the palm-thatch roof, then carried tall glasses of ginger beer to a nearby table of laughing islanders.

"You can have Guadeloupe. I'll take Sabado any day," Ben said. "It's hard to believe we were here just this morning, then on Guadeloupe, and now we're back again, and it's still the same day."

"I wish we had seen my father when we picked up the scuba gear," Jeri said, handing a crust of bread to Black Dog, who sat waiting for it on top of the low wall beside their table. "I want to tell him what we saw."

"Tomorrow will be soon enough," Ben said, "after we make our dive. We can tell him what we found then, too. If we find anything at all, that is." He was silent for a moment, thinking. "The war canoe — you're sure?"

"I'm positive. If I still had my copy of the research paper done by that anthropologist, I could show you. There was a sketch of it, and what I saw was exactly like his sketch. If we get back to Rotole tomorrow before the library closes, I'll show you."

Ben shook his head. "You know, I looked at that thing, too, but I sure didn't notice any war canoe."

"That was a big glyph, and it would take hours really to look at everything on it. I wouldn't have noticed the war canoe, either, if I weren't already familiar with what it looked like. It was in the center of one of the blocks, surrounded by other designs, but once I picked it out, it was obvious — a long, low boat with one of those crazy devil figures on the front." She leaned forward for emphasis. "Ben, that glyph came from here, from Sabado."

"Morgeaux said it all came from Central America," Ben replied.

Jeri cocked her head and narrowed her eyes. "I don't believe that man."

"Well, he also said all the things in his office had been in circulation for a while, so if the glyph did come from Sabado, maybe it came from here a long time ago and he didn't know it. When the paper you read was written, the temple still contained glyphs of the war canoe, and they're gone now, so maybe Morgeaux is where one of them ended up."

Jeri shook her head. "You saw the walls of the temple, Ben. All the glyphs taken from there were removed in chunks, fragments, none of them any bigger than what could be knocked out with a sledgehammer. The glyph in Morgeaux's office is *huge,* and it's in one piece!"

"Which is the best reason of all not to think it came from here," Ben said. "It's too perfect. Look, I don't know much about Mayan culture, but maybe the main civilizations in Central America also had one of these war canoes. If they did, then Morgeaux could be telling the truth and maybe his glyph did come from there."

"I'm not an expert on Mayan culture, either," Jeri said, "but the man who wrote that paper was. And he said the war canoe was not found in any glyphs except those on Sabado. He also thought there could be ruins that were as yet undiscovered here. He made detailed sketches of the area, which were included at the end of the paper, but the last few pages were missing, and I never saw them. They had been torn out."

"Well, one thing's for sure," Ben said. "We know something funny is going on up there."

Jeri looked at him, her eyes showing both excitement and trepidation. "Yeah. Now all we have to do is find out what."

"We'll sail up there as soon as it's light enough to

see the reef. That'll be at sunrise, which means we probably ought to hit the sack right away, don't you think?"

Jeri nodded. "Early to bed, early to rise."

Outside the circle of lantern light at Trina's, the night was so dark they had to feel their way down the hillside path to the banana dock where they had tied the dinghy. Looking seaward, Ben said, "I should have left *Trike*'s mast light on."

"I'm sure we'll find her," Jeri replied.

Ben stepped down into the dinghy and got the penlight he kept in a zippered compartment. He switched it on to show Jeri where to step.

"Let me run the motor," she said.

"Have at it," he said, moving forward to allow room for her and Black Dog. "I'll try to see where we're going from the bow. Choke half on to start, and take it easy."

He held the penlight for her while she moved the choke lever to where he said and yanked the starter rope. As the outboard popped to life, Ben shoved the dinghy away from the piling.

"Straight out," he said.

Jeri opened the throttle part way, and they headed into the blackness. Ben held the light at the bow, but the beam was so feeble it had little effect.

"Bear to the left," he called, trusting his instincts to guide them to where the trimaran was anchored.

Jeri complied, then, her voice enthralled, said, "Ben, look at this!"

Ben twisted around. The water rolling alongside the dinghy and churning in its wake was glittering an iridescent green, like fireworks underwater.

"Phosphorescent plankton," he said. "It's very common in the Caribbean. When it's stirred up, it gives off light."

"It's beautiful!"

"Yeah," Ben agreed. "I love to look at it."

The dinghy laid a sparkling trail on the dark sea, a ghostly streak that faded behind them, and they watched it in rapt fascination — and to the point of distraction. When Ben finally looked up, the dark shape of one of the moored banana boats loomed suddenly in front of them. He shouted in warning, but it was too late.

Jeri gasped and reacted instantly, throwing the outboard hard over and killing the engine in an attempt to avoid the collision, but the port quarter of the dinghy slid into the banana boat's bow, and the impact threw them both forward, sandwiching Black Dog between them. Black Dog yelped in surprise, and Ben barely managed to avoid being thrown out by catching himself against the wooden hull of the banana boat.

"Are you okay?" he asked in the silence that followed.

"Yes, I think so."

"Black Dog. Is he still aboard?"

"Yeah, he's sort of in my lap. I'm sorry, Ben."

"It's not your fault. I'm the one who was supposed to be watching. The tide swung all the boats around, and I should have known they could be almost anywhere." He fiddled with the penlight, which had gone out when his hand hit the side of the boat. When he got it switched on again, he shoved them away from the moored vessel. Immediately they heard the sound of rushing air.

"What's that?" Jeri asked.

"Oh, nothing much," Ben groaned. "We're just sinking is all." He turned the beam of the penlight on the banana boat. A ten-inch bolt stuck straight out from the bow just above the waterline. "That's what got us," he said in disgust and moved the light up the bow, where there was still another bolt sticking out. "What in the hell are those things doing there?"

"I don't think it matters now, Ben. What are we going to do, sit here until we go down?"

The inflatable dinghy had already lost its rigidity and was now beginning to crumple and fold around them.

"I don't think we can make it to *Trike*," he said, "but I carry a repair kit, so we can patch it here." Drawing them against the banana boat again, he took the dinghy's bowline and stepped out, placing one foot on the bolt that had punched the hole through the fabric of the dinghy and holding on to the one above it. "Unfasten the motor and hand it to me when I get aboard. Then we can haul the dinghy up and fix it on deck."

The two bolts made convenient steps, and a moment later, Ben leaned over the banana boat's bulwark and took Black Dog and the outboard from Jeri, who then climbed up and joined him. As soon as they had the dinghy on the rough wooden decking, he got the repair kit from the zippered compartment and began working on the hole.

"Inflatables!" he fumed. "One of these days I'm going to have a *real* dinghy, one that's made of fiberglass and with a foam core so it'll float, no matter what!"

Jeri held the light while he trimmed the hole and buffed the surface around it. He cut an oval patch, applied glue, and pressed the patch into place.

"Very neat," she complimented.

"I've had a lot of practice," he said, standing up. "It needs to set for a few minutes, and it would help if we had something heavy to place on it."

Jeri played the light over the expansive deck. There was no rubble, no pieces of junk, but against the opposite bulwark was a large tarp-covered shape. Ben crossed to it and lifted the tarp's edge. Jeri swung the beam of light onto the object and jumped back, shrieking in terror.

Clawed arms raised, with blood-covered fangs and horns, the monster seemed to leap out at them. Ben, too, jerked in fright, starting to scramble away, before they realized they were not being attacked.

"That's *it*!" Jeri exclaimed, when she recovered her breath. "That's exactly like what knocked me off the cliff, Ben, the same thing that almost got us in the water."

Ben pulled the tarp back the rest of the way, revealing fully the hideous figure of the demon.

"Maybe," Ben said. "Except that this is about twenty times as big as the thing in the water. It must weigh two hundred pounds." He rapped the demon's chin with his knuckles. "It's carved from solid wood."

Jeri touched it, hesitantly running her fingers over the long, curving fangs and the blood-red eyes. It felt artificial and lifeless, but in the dim beam of the penlight the demon's appearance was so ghastly that even now she had to fight back a shudder. "Whoever made it did a good job," she said. "It's horrible looking!"

"A good job of painting, too. It's highlighted just right," Ben observed. "It could have been done by a native craftsman. A lot of these islanders are really talented at carving."

"I wonder what it's doing on a banana boat," Jeri said, placing her hand on it again. She pointed to a hole in the wood below the demon's throat. "Ben, what do you think this is for? And here's another above the horns."

Ben looked at the two holes, noting the distance between them. Moving the heavy sculpture around, he examined the back, which was V-shaped. A large wedge had been cut out of it from top to bottom.

"It goes on the bow!" he said suddenly. "That's what those two bolts are for. They fit through the holes." He wrestled the sculpture back around. "Look! You can see where nuts have been tightened down against the wood! It's a figurehead. That's what this thing is — a removable figurehead!"

"The 'devil ship,'" Jeri said, "the ship that ran down the French couple's yacht, the boat that Black Dog was on." She shook her head. "But it's only a banana boat."

"Maybe not," Ben replied, picking up a block of wood and carrying it to the dinghy to place on the patch. "Let's have another look."

They went the length of the broad deck and searched in the cockpit at the stern but found nothing else unusual. Then Ben lifted the hatch to the engine compartment and took the penlight below. Jeri watched him standing at the bottom of the ladder, looking around. A moment later, he whistled softly in amazement.

"Come take a gander at this," he said.

Jeri climbed down and joined him. At first she didn't see what he was talking about; she had expected something as striking as the figurehead. And then she saw the heavy electrical wiring and the multiple banks of batteries, dozens of them.

"It's been converted to a hybrid," Ben said, walking aft between the rows of batteries, "and I'd say it's a very sophisticated job, too."

"A hybrid?"

"Yeah." He placed a hand on one of two large in-line electric motors. "Instead of being driven by a standard internal-combustion marine engine, it's powered by electricity from the storage batteries. And the batteries are kept charged by that." He pointed the beam of light at a large gasoline generator. "Compliments of SeaCon, no doubt, as is everything else in here — the wiring, the batteries, the motors. All this stuff was on the list of missing inventory."

"What's the point?" Jeri asked.

Ben shook his head and continued to look around. "I don't know, but from the size of these motors, I'd say this heavy old tub would move at a pretty good clip, and unless the generator was running, it would be almost silent, too." Reaching up, he spun the blades on one of a pair of overhead fans.

"What are those for?" Jeri asked.

"To vent this place. They're ducted to the outside. These are lead-acid batteries, and when they're being charged, they release hydrogen. If it wasn't vented to the outside, it could build up and a spark could cause an explosion." He looked around again and nodded. "Yeah, I'd say the whole system was pretty well thought out."

"Who would go to the trouble of doing this to a banana boat?" Jeri asked. "It seems like such a complicated arrangement just to haul bananas a few hundred yards."

"Remember when we were at Trina's watching them load the bananas? One of the boats wasn't being used."

"That's right," Jeri said. "And the waitress said it belonged to someone else, someone who had done a lot of work on it but didn't haul bananas with it anymore."

"This has to be the boat she was talking about."

"So what *is* it used for, other than running down yachts?"

"Your guess is as good as mine," Ben said, motioning with the beam of light for her to head up the ladder.

Topside, Black Dog was waiting patiently by the collapsed dinghy. Replacing the block of wood, they covered the figurehead with the tarp, and Ben reinflated the repaired dinghy with the foot pump.

A few minutes later, all eyes forward, they motored slowly and unerringly through the dark to *Trike*.

Fourteen

A midmorning breeze stirred, and *Trike* began to swing downwind, slowly straightening the loop in her anchor line. Sipping the last of a cup of hot tea, now barely warm, Jeri stood outside the coaming at the stern and looked across the glare on the rippling water to the cliff. Beyond, in the shadow of the tall *gommier* trees, she made out the tip of the pyramid. The setting was tropical and beautiful, peaceful, yet she felt heavy with a sense of foreboding.

Ben emerged from the companionway with a weight belt, which he placed amid the clutter of scuba gear already in the cockpit. "That's everything," he said, looking around. "Tanks, regulators, masks, weights, light, flippers, the works." He looked at Jeri and saw the serious expression. "Having second thoughts?"

She picked up Black Dog with one hand, tucking

him under her chin and holding him with a picture of the affection she felt for him. "I'm suddenly beginning to wonder what we're doing here, Ben. I keep thinking we should have gone on back to Rotole to tell my father about that lawyer guy, Morgeaux, and about the banana boat with the weird figurehead and all the electrical stuff stolen from SeaCon. Instead, here we are at this crazy place again, chasing what?"

"A light we saw in the sea."

Jeri nodded. "Yeah, but something else, too. The figurehead on the banana boat last night was only a block of wood. But that . . . that *thing* was *alive!*"

"We can head back to Rotole right now if you'd rather we didn't make this dive. Whatever it was, it scared me as badly as it did you. Maybe worse," he admitted.

She shook her head, thinking about it, then said, "After going to so much trouble, it doesn't make any sense to back out now."

A few minutes later, they were ready. Laden with the heavy gear, Ben descended the boarding ladder into the water, where the tank and weight belt became weightless. At the top of the ladder, Jeri paused and looked down at him.

"I keep thinking about a real old movie I saw on the late show one night on television. There was this monster that lived in the water. . ."

"*The Creature from the Black Lagoon.* It was a classic." Ben grinned, put his mouthpiece between his teeth, adjusted his face mask, and went under.

They glided downward, Jeri to one side and a few

feet behind him, the rhythmic pull of air and release of bubbles obscuring the normal underwater clicking sounds that rattled constantly in the ears of a free diver. Again, the view of coral and the variety of sea life was of incomparable color and beauty. Thirty feet down, they crossed the expanse of staghorn coral. Then, as they neared the cliff, the coral and bottom receded, falling away to bluish depths. Ben hesitated, then pointed upward, and they surfaced a hundred feet from the face of the cliff.

"It's deeper here than I thought, and I lost my bearings underwater," he said. "Where were we when we were looking down at that light?"

Jeri looked at the cliff and tried to remember. "I'm not sure. It was dark then, but I think it was about where we are now, except maybe a little closer in."

Ben nodded, concurring. "Okay, let's go down."

Trailing bubbles at a steep angle and slowing to equalize the pressure in their ears, they descended again. Jeri checked her depth gauge. At seventy feet, deep enough to require decompression if they stayed very long, they reached bottom. This far down only the shorter wave lengths of light penetrated the water, resulting in a blue overcast, but the visibility remained excellent. With Jeri following, Ben kicked along the rock formations at the base of the cliff until they found themselves staring into the black maw of an underwater cave.

The opening was large, at least twenty feet across, and they hovered in front of it for only a moment before Ben unfastened the small diving light attached to his waist and motioned for Jeri to follow. He had already started in before she had time to react, but she surged, catching him quickly and yanking on his flipper. When she had his attention, she pointed into the pitch-black cave and shook her head fiercely. It looked like the perfect residence for the creature that had attacked them, and she had no intention of going in there.

She read the amusement in Ben's eyes, but she was adamant. Even when he indicated with his hands held a short distance apart that they would go in just so far, she still shook her head. Finally, he shrugged and turned, deciding that he would go by himself. Faced with the equally disturbing prospect of waiting outside alone, Jeri blew out a burst of bubbles and reluctantly followed.

The intense darkness was terrifying, and the diving light did little to alleviate the terror. The beam reached to the walls and ceiling and bottom of the cave, but ahead it illuminated only floating bits of plankton and then faded to black. Suddenly a large shape emerged from the darkness, spearing them both with panic. Jeri squawked in horror through her mouthpiece as the thing turned and faced them, but this time there were no horns, no fangs, only the placid face and eyes of a hundred-pound grouper. The fish looked curiously at them, then swam slowly away, leaving them weak from the surge of adrenalin.

Oh lord, Jeri thought. Please, let's *get out of here!* But Ben pushed onward, and too frightened to turn back on her own now, she followed.

Bubbles rolled like inverted beads of quicksilver along the rock above them, indicating that they were moving upward. When Jeri looked behind them, she saw that the entrance had fallen away dramatically. From more than a hundred feet inside the cave, it was far below them and continuing to recede. If the monster came now, there would be no way they could escape it. She hooked a hand onto Ben's weight belt and did not let go.

Cautious at first, Ben grew increasingly impatient to see where the cave went, and Jeri had to kick strongly to avoid slowing them down. But finally she had had enough. They were so far from the entrance that the disk of daylight was little more than a bright dot. Tugging on his belt, she was trying to make him turn back, when without warning they broke through the surface.

It was so startling that for a moment Jeri didn't realize what had happened. In the sudden confusion of losing the resistance of the water and the disruptive sound of their own splashing, she could think only that they were under attack from the monster. She gasped, almost choking on a mouthful of sea water before Ben's voice established reality.

"Wow!" he said, removing his mouthpiece and pushing back his face mask. "Look at this!"

Treading water, he shined the diving light around them. They were in a large circular cavern, a cul-de-sac that was open on one side, leading off into more darkness. From walls to domed ceiling, the rock that surrounded them was covered with intricate glyphs.

119

The ancient carvings-in-stone took virtually all the available space. Hardly a square inch of rock was undecorated.

"What *is* this? Where are we?" Jeri asked in disbelief.

"I don't know," Ben replied, "but we're not the first people to come here."

He turned the light up to the ceiling again. A double row of high-intensity floodlamps hung from wires that trailed off into the darkness.

Fifteen

Ben heaved himself up from the edge of the water and onto the hard smooth rock that comprised the floor of the cave. He gave Jeri a hand and helped her up beside him.

"Look," he said, pointing down into the pool of water. "It must be a hundred meters or more to where we came in, and yet we can still see the light from the outside."

"Then what we saw the other night must have been these lights on the ceiling," Jeri added.

"Yeah. The water's so clear that when they're on they shine all the way down and out into the sea."

Jeri took the light from Ben's hand and turned the beam onto the wall surrounding the pool again. "It's incredible!" she said. "In this one area alone, there are more glyphs than there ever were in all of the part of the temple that's above ground. This would make an archaeologist's mouth water."

On the wall above the opposite side of the pool was a large display of priest-like figures placing the draped body of a woman onto a watery surface. On each side of the woman waited a pair of sharks, their heads up and teeth bared hungrily.

"The Maya are well known to have practiced human sacrifice," she said.

"It may have been what they used this pool for," Ben said. "Sharks would come here, especially if they were used to being fed."

Jeri shuddered, thinking what it must have been like — shadows dancing in the torchlit cave, the normally placid water of the pool churning and turned red as sharks devoured their hapless victim. Moving the light on past the sacrificial stone, Jeri stopped suddenly. "Ben, *there!*"

In the center of the next block of glyphs was a long, narrow boat with the figure of a devil on its bow.

"Is that what you saw in the lawyer's office?"

"It was *identical!*" she said.

"It also looks a little like what that banana boat would look like with the wooden figurehead attached," Ben added. "I wonder if there's a connection."

"There's one connection," Jeri replied. "You can bet that the lights in here and the electrical wiring came from the same place as the electrical equipment on the banana boat — from SeaCon. Let's get out of here, Ben. I'm scared."

"If there was anyone here right now, the floodlamps

would be on," he replied, motioning farther up into the cave with the light. "I think we should try to see where all this goes."

"What if someone comes?"

Ben kicked off his flippers and began removing his tank. "We'll leave our gear here, where we can get to it in a hurry."

Reluctantly, Jeri followed his lead and removed her scuba equipment. A few moments later they began making their way into the higher recesses of the cave.

As in the area around the pool, the sides of the cave were an uninterrupted display of highly detailed glyphs. Although they noticed no repetition of the shark scene, the long "war canoe" was a common theme.

The cave was large, with numerous branches that led into blind alleys. These, too, were covered with glyphs, and in one branch, the entire wall was an enormous fresco. Mineral seepage had obliterated much of it, but the depiction of a raid or war, possibly with Carib Indians, was plainly visible in reds, yellows, and blues.

"Talk about dedication," Jeri said. "Can you imagine the amount of work that must have gone into creating all this?"

"Just getting it ready was a huge undertaking," Ben said, running his fingers over one of the figures of stone. "This was probably a natural cave, and they had to chisel the walls flat before even beginning to put the art on it."

"Think what this could mean to Sabado, Ben. Mayan

ruins are a terrific draw for tourists, and this place —
it's utterly fantastic!"

"Tourists," Ben said in a tone that indicated he didn't
think much of the idea.

"Food and medical care," Jeri said. "And schools.
This could help provide all that if it was managed
right."

"Somebody's already managing it," Ben said, looking again at the double row of floodlamps running the
length of the ceiling. "The question is who — and
why."

"Yeah," Jeri replied, her voice tense. "I just hope
we don't meet the who."

They turned into another of the deep alcoves, and
again they found both sides and the end decorated
with blocks of glyphs. Looking quickly, they returned
to the main part of the cave. Three hundred feet from
where they had come up out of the water, the main
passageway made an abrupt bend. Leading with the
light, Ben turned the corner and froze. Jeri bumped
into him and shrieked at what she saw.

A hideous and slimy face stared up at them from the
floor of the cave. Curved fangs sprouted from the corners of its oozing mouth, and for a split second they
expected the monster to lunge at them, but it remained strangely still. Then they saw that one of its
horns was bent out of shape, and the eyes were oddly
vacant. Still holding his breath, Ben reached out with
his bare foot and nudged the thing with his toe. It fell
away from the side of the cave and flopped over. Jeri
jumped.

"Rubber!" Ben exclaimed, reaching down and picking the thing up. "It's nothing but a mask!" He turned it over, revealing a diving mask that was bonded inside the back of it. He slipped the straps over his head, pulled it down and turned to Jeri. "Here's our monster, guaranteed to scare your pants off if it comes up out of the water at you at night!"

"And there's its arm," Jeri said, pointing to another object leaning against the side of the cave.

Ben picked that up, too, an extension with a plastic claw at one end and a grip that fit his hand at the other. Growling, he advanced menacingly at her.

"You look like a sick Halloween joke," she said.

Ben removed the mask and dropped it and the phony claw to the floor of the cave. Nearby was also a pair of flippers. "All you'd have to be is a reasonably strong swimmer and you could scare two people in a dinghy half to death."

"But what about the noises we heard?"

"We'll see if we can find that out, too," Ben replied, shining the light still farther in the cave.

"Here's one of the noises," he said, picking his way around a freshly cut stack of lumber to an industrial-quality table saw straddling a mound of sawdust, "and another of the larger items that were on SeaCon's list of missing inventory. This thing makes quite a howl, cutting a board."

"And if it was muffled way inside this cave and way out on the tip of an island, in the middle of nowhere, it could sound pretty scary, especially to anyone who's superstitious," Jeri said.

"And even to a couple of people who aron't superstitious," Ben reminded her.

Resting on a layer of sawdust nearby was a two-by-four-foot section of glyphs. The stone slab was two inches thick, and the corners had been cut perfectly square. Beside it were a dozen or more other slabs of glyphs, each wrapped in burlap and crated in an individually constructed wooden form.

"The place is being looted, Ben! These priceless works of art are being *stolen*! Somebody is selling Sabado's cultural treasures! And people like that Morgeaux creep are buying!"

Ben picked up an air-driven nail gun that lay on the floor beside the stack of glyphs. He followed the air line back to a big compressor, and from the compressor, they followed a pair of air hoses down the cave and into another of the offshoots. Attached to the ends of the hoses were air-driven cutting tools fitted with diamond-edged blades.

In here, the side of the cave had been marked off in a chalk grid, and there were huge sections of sheer, sliced walls, where slabs of glyphs had been excised from the rock like pieces of veneer.

"They intend to take it all, don't they?" Jeri said. "Start at this end and not stop until every last piece is gone!"

"That's what it looks like," Ben replied, "and I'd also say they're going about it pretty efficiently. It may take a little while, but I bet they could get most of it within six months or a year. And because they've got the equipment to cut it out in big unbroken pieces, I'd also bet they're able to get a good price for it!"

Jeri nodded. "And keeping it a secret has been easy for them. I learned from back issues of the local newspaper that the islanders have been superstitious of this area for many years. Most people stay away from here, and any odd goings-on that they did see or hear would be attributed to the work of demons, which would make them even more likely to stay away."

Returning to the main part of the cave, they found the generator that supplied the electricity for the equipment and lights. It was set up beside a wide flight of steps, which were part of a stairway sculptured into the stone, descending from the ceiling.

"The entrance," Ben said. "We must be near the temple, or possibly even beneath it."

In the ceiling at the top of the steps was a narrow groove, delineating a rectangular opening in the stone the same width as the stairway. Obviously it was the intended way into and out of the underground corridors of glyphs, but the massive "door" was closed, and it looked as solid and impenetrable as the stone ceiling itself.

"There must be some way of moving that from the other side," Ben said. "A couple of fancy hydraulic jacks missing from SeaCon's inventory were capable of lifting several tons, so that may be where they ended up."

Jeri pointed to the center of the steps. A path of footprints was plainly visible in the fine layer of dust produced by the cutting tools. "It looks well used," she said, "and recently."

"Then that accounts for just about everything," he said, turning to her. "The 'monster' that pushed you off the cliff and came after us in the dinghy was somebody's idea to frighten us away from here, and all the strange noises — the screams, the howls, and the hissing sound — were caused by machines cutting wood or rock or the compressor running or releasing air."

"Sounds that also help keep people away from here," Jeri said, "so that whoever's doing this can go about their looting without interference."

"Right," Ben agreed. "They cut the glyphs off the walls, pack them, then haul them away to sell." He turned the light back toward the stack of crated glyphs. "But, you know, those things are heavy, and there's no road up here. I wonder — "

"The banana boat!" Jeri said quickly.

"Of course!" Ben exclaimed. "It's got a shallow draft for maneuvering through shoals and coral, and since it's powered by electricity, it could move up and down the coast at night and nobody would even hear it."

"And if anybody saw it, the figurehead might make them think it was some kind of ghost ship, or 'devil ship,' especially at night, and that might scare them away from it, too."

"Then, once the glyphs are loaded on the banana boat, it heads out to sea. Probably the banana boat is just used as a tender to carry the glyphs to another boat waiting offshore."

"Then the banana boat returns to its anchorage at Laudat, where they remove the figurehead, and by the time the sun comes up it's just sitting at anchor by the other banana boats, and no one's the wiser," Jeri said.

Ben nodded. "A very neat operation. Now the only thing remaining is to figure out who's behind it."

They began a systematic search of the area, trying to make sure they looked at everything in the beam of light. Near where the glyphs were being crated, they found two papers that were folded lengthwise and sticking out from between the side of the cave and a section of crating that was leaning against it. While Ben held the light, Jeri unfolded the thicker one and flipped through its pages.

"It's the copy I made of the anthropological study by that guy from the University of Texas!" Jeri exclaimed in surprise. "It was in my pack!" Near the end of the paper, a phrase leaped out at her. "Listen to this, Ben! 'Although there are apparent similarities between the hieroglyphs found on Sabado and those of the Central American Maya, the low volume of evidence left by such a small family may never be sufficient to prove the connection beyond all doubt.' "

Ben shrugged. "So?"

"That phrase, 'small family.' Those are the same words that creep Morgeaux used when he referred to the Maya of Sabado. It could be a coincidence, but I bet he's read this paper, too, Ben. And if he has, then he's not just a *buyer* of art stolen from here. He's involved; maybe even behind it."

"It would make sense," Ben agreed. "Especially since he works for SeaCon. He'd be in the right position to put together something like this. And as an attorney and a collector, he'd probably know how to go about marketing it." He handed her the other paper. "What's this?"

There were three pages, and all were well worn from having been folded and refolded. As soon as Jeri spread them out and saw the detailed sketches, she realized what they were. The holes at their left edges were ripped out, confirming it.

"Remember I told you some of the pages were missing at the end of the study when I read it at the library? Well, these are the missing pages," she said.

The sketches were drawn to scale and were topographical maps of the area that surrounded the temple. The University of Texas researcher had made careful measurements of the ground, its contours, and, with the exception of trees and vegetation, had plotted all objects that were located on it. In annotations and footnotes, he had made suggestions as to which areas he thought were likely sites for productive digs, the most interesting of which he considered to be a triangular section of ground directly behind the temple.

"Look at this," Jeri said, tracing her finger around the dotted line, which encompassed sketches of three separate rock formations, marked A through C. Then she went to the footnote: " 'The ratios of relative distances and masses among these three monoliths indicate a relationship suggestive of the following: Object A was at one time movable by a lever whose fulcrum was Object B and whose counterweight was Object C. The implications are that the subsurface at Object A may be worthy of investigation.' "

" 'Object A,' " Ben said. "That's the big rock right behind the temple, isn't it?"

"Yeah. It's where I was eating lunch when I first saw *Trike*'s mast, but I've never seen the other two, 'B' and 'C'," she said.

Ben looked at the sketch, trying to relate it to what he remembered. "That area's all grown over with vines."

"That's right," Jeri agreed. "The vines grow all the way up to one corner of the temple."

"Then if 'Object A' moved, or lifted up, which it would have done if the lever was placed where he says, the lever could have been wooden, say a tree trunk, which would have rotted away a long time ago. Yeah," Ben said, "it looks plausible all right. You pry up 'A',and there are the stairs coming down into here."

"So somebody else found this paper before I did and went on to prove its author right," Jeri said.

"Unfortunately," Ben replied.

Jeri returned the papers to where they had found them and was starting to suggest that they get out of here, when a noise, a single *clunk*, jumped out from the darkness around them.

"Ben!" she whispered, squeezing his arm.

There was a grating sound, and a shaft of light pierced the blackness above the stairway.

"Go!" Ben said, and they turned, fleeing through the dark as a foot appeared on the top step.

They turned the corner and raced down the main length of the cave. Seconds later, the generator started up, and the cave exploded with light, blinding the two teenagers.

"Run!" Ben hissed.

"Just get your weight belt and mask on!" he urged when they reached the pool. "Stick your regulator in your mouth and jump in holding your tank! We'll put them on when we're underwater!"

"Oh Ben!" Jeri said nervously, her hands shaking so much they seemed to be defeating her. She thought she heard the scuff of steps on the cave floor, and she was consumed by panic. "Just get this thing on! Get it on! *Get it on!*" she told herself.

"Hurry!" Ben said, but she was ahead of him, getting her weight belt around her waist while he was still retrieving his.

Cinching the belt, Jeri pulled her mask over her face. She turned and reached for her tank, but jumped back in surprise as a husky Sabadoan ran into view. He saw them and stopped suddenly, grinning.

Behind him appeared SeaCon's construction foreman, Brocker. The big man moved rapidly and was upon them before Jeri could raise the regulator to her mouth. Then he stopped.

In Brocker's right hand was a .45 automatic, and on his face was a look of satisfaction.

Sixteen

A crab ambled by, and Jeri drew her legs up in case it intended to examine her toes. The movement sent the crab scurrying.

Jeri could see where the hemp bindings were sinking into the flesh above her ankles. Her wrists were tied just as tightly behind her. She flexed her fingers, her hands straining for circulation.

"I feel like gangrene's beginning to set in," she said to Ben, who sat in the same shape beside her.

"Me, too," he replied and shifted his weight in a futile attempt to find a more comfortable position on the cold hard stone. "But something tells me they don't much care."

A few minutes later, when one of the two Sabadoans who had come to the cave with Brocker brought the scuba gear and dumped it in a heap nearby, Ben complained about the way they were tied. But the man ignored them, going instead to join Brocker and the other Sabadoan in the corridor, where the screeching of tools and expulsion of dust indicated they were cutting more glyphs from the wall.

"What are they going to do with us?" Jeri asked.

He shook his head. "I don't know, but we shouldn't have hung around for so long."

"Yeah, I know," sighed Jeri.

"You know," said Ben, "all the time I was working around him, there was something about Brocker that bothered me. I couldn't put my finger on it, but now I know what it is. He's cold-blooded. It's in his eyes."

"You get the feeling that he could watch someone being boiled alive and not even flinch," Jeri agreed. "Strange how I never noticed it in him before. But then I never paid much attention to him before."

"A good man to run an operation like this," Ben said. "The technical knowledge and ability to cut rock."

"And no concern for what he's doing to art whose loss is a tragedy to all mankind," Jeri finished for him.

"Not to mention us," Ben said with gallows humor, "which suddenly seems to me like the loss that would be an even bigger tragedy to mankind; especially to *this* representative of mankind," he added.

"If you're trying to scare me, you're succeeding," Jeri said. "I'd prefer to think they're going to let us go."

"Right," Ben replied, with a total lack of conviction. Marked by the cutting pain in their wrists and ankles and the dust billowing from the corridor where the men were working, the time crept by. The relentless thudding of the compressor and screaming of the tools became a white noise that reverberated through the caves and their heads. When it finally ceased, the silence, by comparison, seemed to envelop the drone of the generator.

The two Sabadoans emerged from the other part of the cave carrying a heavy glyph between them. Brocker followed. Straining, covered with dust and sweat, the Sabadoans laid the slab of stone on a burlap pad. One of them picked up an air hose with a nozzle on the end and blew the dust from the glyph. Then they wrapped the glyph with burlap, tied it with hemp, and were hammering the crating together around it when Fitzgerald, SeaCon's company clerk, came hurrying down the steps into the cave.

Seeing Jeri and Ben, the older man's movements became jerky, nervous. When he reached Brocker, he said, "You got them."

Brocker glanced sideways at him and cursed. "Yeah, no thanks to you. You should have told me the instant you found out they had gotten diver's gear yesterday. We barely got here in time."

"I didn't realize what they were getting it for," Fitzgerald replied defensively.

Brocker was contemptuous of him. "After the trouble they've given us already, a complete fool would have known what they were going to do with it."

When Fitzgerald looked at Jeri and Ben, his gaze was shifty, darting away to avoid eye contact.

Jeri leaned her head toward Ben. "Between the two of them, as foreman and clerk, it's no wonder they were able to steal SeaCon blind and get away with it."

Brocker walked over and stood towering in front of them. His look was cold. "You should have gotten your butt out of here while you had the chance, boat drifter," he said to Ben.

"What are you going to do with us?" Jeri demanded.

Brocker turned to Fitzgerald as if he was the one who had asked the question. "When we haul this shipment out tonight, we'll take them with us. We'll tow the kid's boat down island and let the current put it on the reef. When the pieces and bodies wash up, it'll look like they made the serious mistake of trying to sail this coastline at night."

Fitzgerald looked shocked, but not because murdering two people was a moral issue with him. His concern was only for his own skin. "Are you sure it'll work?"

"You got a better idea?" Brocker snarled.

Fitzgerald shook his head nervously. "Morgeaux said it will take some time for him to dispose of these. So after you make the shipment tonight and, uh, take care of other matters, we can close down the operations up here for a few weeks until everything blows over."

"Brilliant," Brocker replied sarcastically.

"What time do you meet the ship offshore?" Fitzgerald asked.

"Midnight. We'll be finished here in another hour,

and as soon as it's dark, we'll bring the boat around and start getting it loaded."

"You won't get away with this," Jeri said, her voice more shaky than defiant. "My father — "

" — will think he should have used better judgment than to trust his daughter to a young man so foolish as to try to sail in dangerous waters at night," Fitzgerald said, checking his watch. A moment later, he left in a hurry, disappearing at the top of the flight of stone steps into the outside world.

Brocker and the two Sabadoans went back for the last of the glyphs they had cut, leaving Jeri and Ben alone again. They exchanged solemn looks, then Jeri twisted, leaning her head on his shoulder.

"I have this numb feeling," she said, "as if my mind is trying to protect me from what it thinks it heard."

Ben took a deep breath and let it out slowly.

After packing the last slab of glyphs, the larger of the Sabadoans picked up one of the razor-edged machetes that virtually all Sabadoan males carried and walked slowly, deliberately toward them. There were streaks on his muscular body where sweat had washed away the dust, and when Jeri looked into his eyes, she was electrified with new terror. She saw a kind of cruelty that was the equal of Brocker's, and she knew this was the man who had posed as a monster, shoving her from the cliff and attacking them in the dinghy.

To him, she was the pampered, spoiled offspring of an American professional, a wealthy outsider, now granted authority over people like him. In this man's mind, whatever happened to her was what she deserved.

Jeri looked away, trying to conceal the fear that sent her heart racing.

The Sabadoan reached out with the machete, and she felt its cold point against her cheek. He pressed with the tip of the blade, forcing her to face him again, and then he turned the machete under her chin, tapping with the flat side, toying with her, the point at the curve of her throat, depressing her flesh.

Jeri's mouth went dry.

With pressure barely light enough to avoid cutting her, he traced the edge of her windpipe. He drew the machete through the hollow in her throat, over her collarbone, and down between her breasts, where he let the point rest against the fabric of her swimsuit top. He smiled, almost as if he were on a drug. Her fear was his pleasure. She tried to swallow but could not. Her throat felt paralyzed.

Her reprieve came only because Brocker appeared behind the Sabadoan. "Are you through here?" he asked.

"Done," the man said and withdrew the machete slowly, reluctantly, without taking his eyes from Jeri as he did so.

"Then let's clear out," Brocker ordered. Bending over the scuba gear, he removed the regulators and opened the tanks' valves. The air blasted out in a loud hiss, and the valves turned icy with frost.

"If you get yourself untied while we're gone, it won't do you any good," Brocker said. "The door to this place can't be moved from the inside, and without air, you'll drown before you get halfway out the way you came in."

The three men left, shutting off the generator. When the massive stone door was lowered back into place, Ben and Jeri were cast into darkness that was as black as death.

Seventeen

"He's right, you know," Ben said in the dark.

"Who?"

"Brocker. I should have left Sabado while I had the chance. I should have left with the first wind. Then neither of us would be in this fix."

"I wouldn't have let you go," Jeri said.

"Yes, you would have. You would have stood on the dock, waving, looking sad of course, but letting me go all the same. And even having Black Dog, I was going to feel the loneliest I had ever felt in my life."

"You could have asked me to go with you," she said.

"I couldn't. I would have had to hear you say no."

"How could I have ever said no?"

For several moments they were silent, each thinking what might have been. Being free on the open sea seemed wonderful beyond belief.

"Come on," Jeri said finally, scooting around, turning her back to him. "Let's try to untie each other's wrists. That's the way they always do it in the movies."

"If your wrists are tied as tight as mine, it's not going to be that easy," he said. "I can hardly feel anything with my fingers anymore. But we better give it a try. In fact, we better give *everything* a try."

They aligned their backs and bent forward, fingers playing over one another's bindings. Their wrists had been wrapped repeatedly with narrow hemp. Hemp also ran between their arms and was knotted several times. Merely identifying the knots was difficult enough; untying them with numb, clumsy fingers in awkward positions was impossible.

"It's useless," Ben said after nearly half an hour of trying. "We need something to cut it with. There are all kinds of sharp things in here, but we need to be able to move around to find something."

"If I could get my hands in front of me, I think I could untie my ankles," Jeri said. "There's only one knot, and it's on top."

Ben heard her squirming around. "What are you doing?"

"Normally I can hold my hands together and put my body through my arms. I'm pretty flexible. But the way my wrists are tied there's not nearly as much room inside my arms." She grunted as she struggled. "Damn!"

"What's the matter?"

"It's my butt! I've got my butt halfway through, and it won't go any farther. It's killing my wrists! It feels

141

like it's cutting my hands off. And I'm also about to break my arms!"

Her hair brushed against Ben's fingers. "What is your head doing down there?" he asked.

"I . . . I'm . . . lying . . . on my side," she grunted, "trying to get my . . . butt through. Darn! I wish it was like Sunie Marchbanks' butt."

"Who is Sunie Marchbanks?"

"A girl I went to high school with. She had the teeniest little rear end you ever saw! Okay!" she said, letting her breath out. "I made a little progress. Now a little more. Oh great!" she said in disgust. "That's just great!"

"What?"

"My arms are stuck on my swimsuit bottom!" She twisted, drawing her knees up to her chin and trying to coax her shoulders into giving another fraction of an inch toward her hips. "Okay, moving again," she said. "Of course my swimsuit's going down, too! Lucky for me it's so dark in here."

"It's okay. I wouldn't be offended."

"There! I'm out! Hands in front of me!" She struggled to a sitting position. "Boy! the floor's cold!"

Between the fingernails of her thumb and forefinger, she tugged at the knot at her ankles until the hemp loosened. Then she quickly removed it and got to her feet.

"Our scuba gear is straight across from us," Ben said. "I think the light was dropped on top of everything else."

Jeri could see nothing in the pitch black, but she

found the gear, no trouble: she nearly fell over one of the tanks as she shuffled forward. Finally she located the small underwater light. Holding it cupped in her bound hands, she switched it on. Flashing the beam of light around the immediate area, she said, "They were cutting the burlap with something."

"A utility knife," Ben replied. "Check the toolbox where they were working."

The toolbox was only a few steps away, and the utility knife lay on top of the other tools. Jeri picked it up, holding it against the light between her hands, then went down on her knees in front of Ben. "If you'll hold it between your legs, so I can see . . ."

She put the light between his knees, and he clamped it there. "Heck," Ben said, sounding disappointed now that he could see her. "You got your swimsuit back up."

"It was either that or fall on my face when I tried to walk," she said, holding the handle of the utility knife between her own knees and bending forward, guiding her wrists over the razor edge, which pushed easily through the hemp. Her hands broke apart, free.

Hurrying, she cut away the bindings at Ben's ankles, but behind his back, she had to work more carefully. The rope was recessed so deeply into his flesh it required patience to avoid cutting him. When his hands were finally free, they both sat rubbing their wrists.

"Even the relief hurts," Jeri said now that she could allow herself to feel the blood returning to her fingers. She turned the light on Ben's hands and gasped when she saw blood oozing from the deep marks on one wrist. "Oh Ben!"

"It's okay," he said, grimacing as he bent and stretched dark, purplish fingers. "I was afraid they were going to fall off, but they're coming back to life now. I can actually feel them." He drew her wrists into the light and pressed gently around the grooves in her flesh. "Yours are bad, too, but I think we'll both live."

"Not unless we find some way to get out of here before they get back," Jeri said solemnly.

Ben got to his feet. "They said they were going to bring the banana boat around after dark. That's not very long from now. We better figure out something fast."

It took only a few minutes to be convinced that Brocker had told them the truth. There was no going out the same way the men had. According to the sketches, the stone that closed the entrance at the top of the stairway would have weighed several tons.

"There's nothing in here that we could use to move it," Ben said, running his hand along the underside of the stone.

"Then that leaves the other end of the cave," Jeri said.

They went the length of the cave and stood staring into the pool. The light from the outside world was now so faint it was barely discernible through the shaft of water.

"The sun's going down, and twilight is brief in the

tropics," Ben said. "It's going to be dark outside in a few minutes."

"How long do you think it will take them to bring the boat around?"

"Not more than an hour. Considerably less if it has much speed."

"Those big motors and batteries . . ."

"Yeah, it looked fast all right," Ben agreed. Then he nodded toward the water. "I can at least give it a try."

"What?" Jeri asked incredulously. "Free dive that?" She shook her head. "No way. It can't be done."

"Better to try it than just sit and wait for them to come back for us."

"It's more than seventy feet deep where we came into this cave, Ben. South Pacific pearl divers rarely dive deeper than fifty or sixty feet, and nobody can free dive as well as they can. They also use rocks and go straight down. You can't do that: you'd have to travel hundreds of feet at an angle first."

He turned the light on her and affected a tone of wonder. "Any other facts you have to discourage me, Miss *Book of Knowledge*?"

"Yes, the most important one of all. If you were to try to free dive out, that means you'd be leaving me in here by myself, and there's no way I'm going to allow that!" She put her hands to her head, trying to control a surge of fear. "Ben, what are we going to *do*?"

He tried to sound calm and analytical. "If we can't get out of here, we can at least try to ambush them when they come back. With all the tools around here, we should be able to come up with some kind of weapon."

Jeri could think of only one weapon: the machete the big Sabadoan carried. She didn't want to go up against that. "There has to be some way we can get out," she said, looking into the pool again. "Ben, all we'd need is a few minutes of air, right?"

"Yes, but the tanks are completely empty. There's not a breath in either of them."

"What about the compressor? Could we use it somehow to put some air in them?"

"Maybe," he said, picking up quickly on the idea. "The fittings that go with the tools won't mate to the valve on the tanks, but maybe we can rig something. It's worth a try!"

The pressure in the big tank that served as a reservoir to the compressor had bled down, and the gauge indicated there was less than twenty pounds per square inch remaining.

Ben did some rough calculations. "To be able to draw a breath at seventy feet will require at least thirty-five to forty pounds of pressure. And we'll use a lot of air just getting down that far. We're going to need about a hundred pounds of air in our tanks to make it."

Ben walked over to the generator, switched on the ignition and pushed the starter button. The engine came to life. He pulled the main lever on the circuit box, and the lights came on, blinding and white. The compressor began pounding.

"Wait, Ben! They'll see the light in the water like

we did!" Jeri said. "And they'll know we're not tied up!"

Hurriedly opening the circuit box, Ben began shutting down breakers, until only the short bank of lights directly above the compressor remained on. These were not bright enough to shine around the bends of the cave and illuminate the distant pool of water. Then, disconnecting a section of air hose, he held the open end of the coupling against the mouth of a scuba tank k-valve and had Jeri turn the main valve at the compressor.

It didn't work. Air blasted out from where the two ill-fitting surfaces met, and no matter how tightly he tried to hold them together, the seal was inadequate to pressurize the scuba tank.

"Maybe the hose will do better by itself," he said, cutting off the brass fitting with the utility knife and jamming the end of the hose against the scuba valve. "Open it up."

This time the tank began to pressurize, but only for a moment. The hose blew out of Ben's hand and whipped away. He retrieved it and tried again, but it was useless.

"I can't hold them together by hand. We'll have to try something else."

"If we could just get enough air into one tank, we could 'buddy breathe' long enough to get out of here," Jeri said.

"Yeah," Ben replied, thinking. "So maybe we could use the line from one tank to help fill the other."

Ben cut through the high-pressure line to one of the

regulators with a hacksaw and attached the fitting at one end to the tank. The regulator's line was smaller than the hose from the compressor but not small enough to fit one inside the other. So, again, the only way to connect them was to butt the two surfaces together.

"If we had some electrician's tape, we'd stand a chance," Ben said.

"Tape, tape, tape!" Jeri repeated, and they both went into a frenzy, searching among the toolboxes and various pieces of machinery. But in spite of the large amount of electrical wiring present, they couldn't find even a single roll of common black plastic tape. All they accomplished was to waste precious time.

Finally, Ben picked up a plastic wrapper that one of the blades for the cutting tools had come packaged in. He squared the edges of the plastic with the utility knife, then wrapped it carefully around the junction of the two air lines. While Jeri held the plastic in place, he whipped the joint with hemp.

"Ben, hurry!" Jeri pleaded.

"Done!" he said, tying it off. "Cross your fingers!"

Jeri slowly opened the valve to the compressor, and air rushed through the line. The crude joint leaked immediately, but pressure began building in the scuba tank. It was approaching a usable amount, when a bubble of plastic rose between the hemp and blew out. Quickly, Ben closed the valve on the scuba tank to save as much air as possible, but he shook his head in disappointment.

"It's not enough. This won't work."

The compressor built 250 pounds of pressure in its large storage tank and shut off. In the comparative silence Jeri and Ben stood looking at each other in dejection.

"It's after dark by now," Ben said. "We're running out of time."

Jeri placed her hand on the large steel tank of the compressor and said with desperate wistfulness, "It's too bad we can't just use this like it is."

Ben looked at her, then raised the heel of his hand to his forehead and clamped it there. "Of course!" he exclaimed. "We *can* use it. Just like it is! Why didn't I think of it before? Hurry! All the air hose — get every length!"

Racing into the darkened corridors, they unsnapped air hoses from the cutting tools and gathered two additional coils of hose that had not been in use.

"Turn on the flashlight," Ben said, disconnecting the compressor from its power source and killing the generator. The cave was thrown into blackness again.

Like a two-wheeled wheelbarrow, the compressor was portable, but it also weighed almost six hundred pounds. Ben took the handles and strained against its inertia, pushing. With coils of air hose slung over both shoulders, Jeri pulled from the front and kicked debris out of the way of the wheels as they rolled the compressor forward. When they reached the pile of diving gear, they stopped to string face masks and fins on weight belts, which they laid across the top of the compressor.

The task of moving the heavy machine got suddenly

easier after they made the turn. On the sloping floor, the compressor unit rolled downhill effortlessly. To keep it under control, Ben leaned back on the handle and let the skids drag against the stone, but still it seemed to take forever to reach the pool, which was absolutely dark when they arrived there.

Ben rolled the compressor as close to the pool as possible and connected an end of one of the long coils of hose to the outlet at the tank. While he connected all the hoses into a single length and threw it into stacks of figure eights, Jeri got their gear ready.

"Okay," Ben said, snapping the air nozzle onto the end of the hose, "let's get the gear on. Once we're in the water, we won't be able to use the light. If they're outside, they might see it. But we shouldn't have much trouble making our way. All we'll have to do is keep going downhill, and the weight belts will make sure we do that."

"Then as soon as we're out of the cave, we drop the belts and start up," Jeri said.

"Right." Ben turned the light on the pressure gauge. "There's plenty of air in the tank, so let's go through a dry run. Here, hold the nozzle with your fingers over the lever like you're going to squeeze it."

Jeri did as he said, and Ben placed his hand around hers. "When you want air, put the end of the nozzle in your mouth and squeeze. I'll do the same thing when I want a breath, but I'll squeeze your hand, too. That way, we can both keep our hands on it, and each of us will always know where it is."

"Try now?"

"Yeah, but remember, the air's not going to be at the right pressure like it is when it comes out of a regulator. So take it easy. Don't squeeze too hard."

Jeri put the end of the nozzle in her mouth and squeezed. The blast of air nearly burst her cheeks.

"God!" she exclaimed, jerking it away, "I think I just blew my tonsils into my stomach!"

Ben tried but did only a little better. He clearly wasn't expecting the sudden blast of air that he got. He tried again and, after several attempts, had the feel for it. "It's got a hair trigger, but it'll work," he said, passing the nozzle back to her.

This time Jeri managed to control it. Handled with a light touch, the nozzle could be made to deliver a small enough stream of air to inflate her lungs comfortably.

"I'm ready when you are," she said.

In the water, they held on at the edge of the pool, and Ben switched off the light, returning them to total blackness.

"Ready?" he asked.

"Ready."

They took a breath and sank, dropping away, the loops of air hose snaking into the water behind them.

The sensation was as if they had entered a dimension of eternal nothingness, and the only protection from becoming a part of it was their physical contact with the air hose and each other. Jeri drew the first breath from the nozzle, and Ben followed, establishing a routine that gave them plenty of air.

Blind, their fins brushing the floor of the cave, the

pressure in their ears alerting them to the increasing depth, they went the direction their weighted bodies wanted to go. But still they wandered off course, repeatedly bumping against the sides of the cave.

The hose had been coming easily, tumbling into the water behind them. Suddenly it stopped. Ben jerked on it, but it did not come. Horrified, both he and Jeri had a simultaneous vision of Brocker standing with his foot on it, the two Sabadoans reaching to pull it back and haul them in like fish at the end of the line. But the retrieve did not come, and when Ben jerked again, the hose fell free.

They hurried, slowing only to release bubbles and take another burst of air. Distance and depth became confusing. Around them was only unending liquid blackness.

Ben's fin touched something other than smooth stone. He reached down and felt the ragged edge of coral, which did not grow in the perpetual darkness of the cave. He pulled Jeri down to it so she could feel, too. Then, tugging at her weight belt, he shouted, "Up! Up!" Underwater, his cry came out garbled, but she understood: they were out of the cave.

Discarding the weight belts gave them immediate buoyancy and, kicking slowly, they began the ascent. The hose stopped again, this time coming to its end. They inflated their lungs with air one last time, then let the hose fall.

They ascended steadily, releasing a continuous stream of bubbles from lungs that stayed fully inflated; the air they contained expanded as the pressure lessened, as if their lungs produced air from nothing.

The blackness became less complete, interrupted by specks of gray, and they broke through the surface into night that was resplendent with sharp points of starlight and a bright sliver of moon.

"We did it!" Jeri said, breathing the words easily as she still held Ben's hand. They were about fifty feet from the face of the cliff, and there was no sign that the looters had returned. "Where do we go? Ashore?"

"Yeah," Ben said. "I don't want to try to get through the coral in *Trike* at night, and it'll be faster on foot anyway. If we can make it to Laudat, we can find a radio."

"I know where the path is," Jeri said.

Swimming parallel to the shore, they headed away from the cliff toward the strata of rock escarpments near sea level.

Then Jeri caught Ben's arm, stopping him suddenly. "Listen!"

They heard a low, soft whine, a kind of mechanical purring. Seaward, *Trike* was a faint blur of white, the only object visible inside the distant surf. Then the trimaran was blocked from view, as the dark shape of another vessel crossed in front of her.

"Ben!"

"Don't move, and they won't see us."

The devil figure of horns and fangs on the bow of the boat glided in from the darkness like a monster floating through air. The boat passed within a hundred feet of them, its electric motors reversing with a murmur that boiled the sea below its transom. From the stern a figure heaved an anchor into the water and payed out line, securing it when only a few feet remained between the figurehead and the slabs of rock on shore. Then he threw a grapple forward, clanging into the rocks, and drew the bow up tightly, fixing the boat's position.

The man laid out a pair of planks that made a level gangway from the bow to the top of a flat boulder. He then picked up an object they identified by the glint of metal as a machete, and went ashore, disappearing into the shadows of the island.

"He's going toward Laudat!" Jeri said.

"Probably to meet Brocker and whoever else is with him. That means we'll have to take the coastal road. It's the long way around, but a few more hours isn't going to make any difference."

"Yeah, at least we'll be away from here," Jeri said in anticipation of the relief she would feel. "Let's go!"

"Wait," Ben said, stopping her. "Let's see if we can't slow them down, too."

"What are you talking about?"

"Their boat," he said, swimming again. "I think they're going to have some unexpected trouble with it."

Approaching from the banana boat's stern, Ben reached high and caught the gunwale. He kicked off his flippers, got his bare feet against the hull above the waterline, and pulled himself up. Jeri let her fins go, too, and as soon as Ben was on deck, he reached down and helped her up beside him.

They went straight for the engine compartment.

Eighteen

Since late afternoon, the Caribbean breeze had been blowing lightly but steadily from the sea, and whenever Black Dog held his nose in the air, scenting, the only smells he received were those that had come with the wind across the many miles of uninterrupted ocean. He could gather no information at all from the direction of the island, and by nightfall he had begun to pace *Trike*'s deck, moving from the stern of one of the outer hulls to the stern of the main hull and then crossing to the stern of the third hull.

In his throat, Black Dog made a whining, chirping noise, so soft it was barely audible. He had been left aboard *Trike* by himself for long periods of time before, but this time something was different, and his inability to smell anything from shoreward had put him on edge.

His acute hearing picked up the whirring of electric engines before the boat began to negotiate the first barriers of coral. Then, in the rush of scents that came on the wind a few minutes later, he recognized a smell that made the hair go stiff along the length of his spine.

As the scent of the man who had attacked Jeri and Ben in the dinghy grew stronger, Black Dog instinctively moved into the cockpit, the level of his eyes just above the coaming. In tense silence, he watched as the electric boat glided by, and when it disappeared into the scentless region downwind, he resumed pacing, more urgently than ever.

Finally, in frustration, he pawed into darkness at the sailboat's stern, hesitating, reaching, then gathering his legs. His weight shifted beyond the point of no return, and he launched away from the boat.

As soon as he struck the water, Black Dog began swimming the quarter mile to shore.

* * *

"That's going to help," Ben said, finding the box of tools against one of the banana boat's timbers. He swept the light around the rest of the engine room, at the banks of batteries, motors, and electrical wiring. "But if we do something obvious, like cutting a wire, they'll just fix it."

"But at least that would slow them down, wouldn't it?" Jeri was anxious to get off the demon ship as quickly as possible, and now Ben was looking around, thinking, while they were in imminent danger of being caught.

When he saw the exhaust fans, he got an idea. Taking a wrench from the tool box, he placed the light where they both could see by it and said, "Take the caps from all the batteries, while I get the blades off these fans. Be careful of the acid!"

Dismayed but obedient, Jeri began popping the caps from the lead-acid batteries. There were a lot of caps — six to a battery — and even though they came off in sets of three's, it took her almost as long to pry them all off as it did Ben to remove the blades from both fans. Her hands shook, slowing her up all the more.

"They're aluminum," he said, cutting one of the fan's blades into narrow strips with a pair of tin snips and handing the pieces to Jeri. "Put as many as you can into each of the cells. They'll react with the electrolyte and weaken the batteries."

Jeri started down the double row of batteries, rapidly dropping in the slivers of aluminum. The instant the aluminum strips hit the acid, the electrolyte began bubbling, sizzling. "What's it doing?" she asked.

"If I remember my chemistry right, it's producing hydrogen." He gave her another handful of slivers.

As the cells were filled with aluminum, the hydrogen escaped with a noise that sounded like hamburgers sizzling on a grill. When all the aluminum was used up, they quickly put the caps back on the batteries, quieting the noisy hissing to a whisper.

"One last thing and we'll get out of here," Ben said.

Jeri groaned quietly, but didn't say a word. She glanced frequently to the cabin door for any sign of the returning Sabadoan. Her heart pounded so loudly in her ears, she was afraid she wouldn't hear him if he came back.

Finding a small piece of discarded wire sticking out of the bilge, Ben cut a short length at an angle and pushed the sharp point into the insulation of the gasoline-powered generator's coil wire. He trimmed off the excess and placed the coil wire back in its position.

"What will that do?" Jeri asked.

"It should arc from the coil wire to the engine block, grounding out the spark plugs. If the generator runs, it'll run rough, and it may take them a while to figure out what's causing it." He took a final look around. "Now let's get out of here."

"Yes, let's!"

They crept forward over the wooden planking of the banana boat's wide deck and stopped at the bow, crouching behind the bulwarks to listen. The stiffening night breeze stirred the foliage that grew in close to the rocks along the shore, and the shadows moved with the swaying of leaves and limbs.

"What do you think?" Ben whispered. "Is anyone there?"

Jeri shrugged. "I don't know."

They made a run for it, crossing the planks to the flat rock that jutted out from shore. At the path behind the rock, they stopped again and crouched, waiting, listening. Finally, running low, they headed up toward the ruins and the coastal road on the other side.

"Ben!" Jeri shrieked his name.

At the side of the path, the big Sabadoan who had piloted the banana boat seemed to materialize from nowhere. His massive frame blocked the way. He grinned sadistically and stepped forward, slashing with the razor-edged machete.

Ben leaped back, the tip of the blade passing so close to his throat that he felt the swirl of air beneath his chin.

The Sabadoan advanced again. Ben felt Jeri behind him, and they gave ground on the narrow path, trying to stay out of reach of the deadly machete.

The man started forward, shoulder and muscle, the machete beginning its arc with the precision of a snake strike. And then, without warning, he seemed to go into an awkward dance.

Grunting in surprise, he jerked sideways. From his feet came the sound of an animal gone mad.

Black Dog attacked with all the savagery he possessed, hurtling into the man's leg and sinking his teeth into the thick muscle of his calf.

The Sabadoan kicked wildly, but Black Dog clamped with teeth and jaws and hung on, tearing deeper into flesh.

Ben reacted and drove forward. He slammed his shoulder into the man's side, and they both sprawled into the vines at the edge of the path. Ben rolled out and scrambled to his feet.

"Run!" he shouted.

Snarling, Black Dog attacked again, biting, then dodged aside as the machete came down like the blade of a guillotine.

With Black Dog running at Jeri's heels, they fled up the path along the edge of the cliff. At the top they raced toward the ruins, then stopped abruptly as a light appeared among the tree trunks and began bouncing rapidly toward them.

"Brocker!" Ben exclaimed.

Behind them, the injured Sabadoan was up and running. He shouted, telling Brocker that Jeri and Ben were between them.

"We're cut off!" Jeri moaned.

"We'll swim for it!" Ben replied. "Try to make it to *Trike!*"

Retracing their steps, they reached the edge of the cliff at almost the exact spot from which Jeri had been shoved before.

"Jump!"

Jeri hesitated. "What about Black Dog?"

"He can take care of himself," Ben replied. "They don't care about him. It's *us* they're going to kill! Jump!"

Jeri started forward, then stopped and scooped up Black Dog. Holding him tightly, she took a final step and leaped. Ben jumped beside her.

This time Jeri was in control of her fall. She struck the water feet first and released Black Dog as they were driven under.

When the bobbing light reached the top of the cliff, they were swimming hard and already beyond the limits of its beam. But a moment later, the light was moving down the path toward the moored banana boat.

"Hurry!" Ben said as they finally reached *Trike*'s anchorage.

Jeri went up the boarding ladder, then turned to catch Black Dog as Ben heaved him over the toe rail. Heart pounding from a combination of fear and exertion, she raced to the anchor line at the bow and strained to pull the boat into the wind.

Within seconds, Ben had brought the engine to life and got the sailboat moving forward, giving her slack. Racing to the bow, he took the line to help break the hook from the coral as the boat passed over it. For an agonizing moment, the anchor hung, resisting them, and then it broke free.

Jeri threw the slack line out of the way, then looked back as Ben hauled the anchor aboard.

"They're coming!"

Leaping over lines and winches, Ben scrambled into the cockpit. He shoved the throttle to its forward peg. But even as the little diesel engine was rattling up to speed, they heard the muted but powerful surge of big electric motors.

Nineteen

Ben had been in and out of the anchorage often enough that he knew the zig-zag route through the treacherous coral, but only by daylight, when he could use reference points on the island to aid him. At night, however, he could make out none of those bearings.

Jeri looked into the expanse of black water ahead of them. "How can you know where you're going?"

His voice was tense. "I can't. I'm guessing."

Where the surf was breaking, washing over long coral escarpments, Ben had the reef's position well in mind. Giant mushrooming coral heads were the real danger. Rising from the sea floor, they often lay hidden within inches of the surface, waiting to take the bottom out of any boat that struck them.

Ben put the helm over again, made a short jog and corrected, hoping he was right. Its diesel auxiliary running at top speed, the trimaran glided quickly through the chop, but behind them, the big banana boat was making three times their speed. It was rapidly overtaking them.

"How can they go through here so fast?" Jeri said, her voice tight with apprehension.

"They've had practice at navigating these waters at night." Ben turned again, anticipating with dread the impact and awful sound of plywood and fiberglass splintering against coral. But once more the three hulls met only water.

Trike kept moving. Ben made another turn and lined up with the break in the outer reef, where the surf dashed itself white over coral barriers on each side.

"Get the sails ready!" he shouted.

The jib was in its bag but already hanked to the forestay. Jeri shook it out and streamed it downwind on the foredeck, then followed the sheets back to the cockpit to make sure they weren't fouled.

Reaching overhead, Ben had partially uncovered the main. Jeri removed the rest of the tie-downs from the boom, threw the main's cover and the jib bag into an open hatch, and dropped into the cockpit beside him. Looking back, she saw that the banana boat had made up more than half the distance that had originally separated them.

"I thought you said the aluminum would weaken their batteries," she said.

"It should," he replied, then added, "but unfortunately it looks like it's not doing it soon enough!"

Jeri made out the shape of the banana boat's figurehead. "Unless something happens, they're going to catch us in about two more minutes!"

"We're going to gain some speed."

"Enough to outrun a power boat?"

Ben shook his head. "I don't know. Here, take the helm. Hold it dead ahead until I get the sails up, then head her forty-five degrees off the wind to starboard to fill the sails. We're going to beat into the wind!"

Passing through the break in the reef, *Trike* began to pitch over the incoming swells, her rigging snapping and ringing against the aluminum mast. Jeri held the heading into the wind, and Ben's hands moved expertly, running the main and jib to the top of the mast. As Jeri swung the bow off the wind, the trimaran surged ahead, riding up over the swells at an angle.

Behind them, the banana boat had closed the distance to less than two hundred feet, and it was still gaining steadily. The big, heavy craft rolled awkwardly in the open ocean, but the tremendous thrust of its engines more than compensated for its ungainliness.

"Can't we go any faster?" Jeri's voice was pleading.

"She'll go faster on a broad reach," Ben replied, now at the helm again, "but we've got to keep beating until there's enough sea room to turn down the coast!"

He yielded a few degrees in direction for an increase in speed, but the effect seemed inconsequential. Plowing through the water with brute force, the banana boat continued to gain on them. Black Dog jumped onto the seat, and Jeri picked him up to keep him out of the way.

The banana boat closed to less than fifty feet. On the foredeck stood the machete-wielding Sabadoan. He shouted something back to Brocker and motioned with the big blade.

"Are they going to try to ram us?" Jeri asked.

Ben nodded, remembering the banana boat's backbone of massive timbers that he had seen when they were belowdecks. "And if they succeed, they'll break us in half!"

Jeri clutched Black Dog and clenched her teeth. *"Do something!"* she murmured.

Ben turned, coming off the wind to a broad reach. The trimaran seemed to shift gears, picking up speed, running at a multihull's best angle, broad-on to the wind.

Almost immediately the banana boat stopped its rapid gain. It hung thirty-five or forty feet behind them, the two vessels matching each other in speed, the trimaran light and quick, the banana boat heavy and powerful.

For long minutes it was difficult to judge if the space between them was growing or shrinking, but gradually it became apparent that the banana boat was in fact still gaining, creeping steadily closer to *Trike*'s stern.

"Two more knots of wind and we'd kiss them goodbye!" Ben said angrily. "Just two more knots!"

The night wind held steady, unwavering. At any other time, Ben would have considered it ideal, the kind of brisk air that *Trike* loved. The trimaran could fly, and she was flying now, but not fast enough.

"Get ready!" Ben shouted, warning Jeri. "We're going to try to outmaneuver them!"

The banana boat came on, rolling from side to side as it powered up the swells and rammed through their crests. Hand braced against the top of the figurehead, the Sabadoan stood at the bow. His pants, one leg ripped to the knee, whipped and fluttered, and the two boats were so close now that Ben and Jeri could see the wrap he had hastily tied around the dog bites.

"Now!" Ben said, when they were less than ten feet from being rammed.

He threw the helm over hard, and *Trike* responded, her stern sliding away as the banana boat came crashing over the swell. The sailboat's shallow keels cut new grooves in the water, and the boat darted suddenly downwind.

Trike lost speed immediately, but the banana boat was unable to match the quickness of her turn. Running all out, the heavy craft had to make a wide circle to change its direction.

Ben threw the helm over again. The engine, which had continued to run, provided the power to complete the turn, leaving the sails to flap wildly, snatching at their sheets.

"Jibe! Jibe!" he shouted. "Stay down!"

The main boom swung, sweeping across the deck and cockpit with enough force to stave in a skull. At the end of its sheet, the boom slammed to a stop on the opposite side of the boat, the big sail tight with air. Ben let fly with the starboard jib sheet, and Jeri hauled in on the port. A moment later they were trimmed broad-on to the wind again, heading in the opposite direction.

By the time the banana boat made the full 180-degree turn, *Trike* had opened up a sizable lead.

"*All right!*" Jeri said.

Ben looked back and shook his head. The banana boat was at full speed and again overtaking them. "All I did was buy us a little more time."

"Then we'll do it again," Jeri said. "And we'll keep doing it until they give up."

"We can't keep doing it," Ben replied. "Maybe once more, but each time we turn downwind, we get closer to the reef. After the next turn, there won't be enough room left to do it again. If we try, we'll end up on the reef, which is just what they want!"

Ben held the heading as long as possible, coaxing all available speed from the combination of sails and wind, but the power of the banana boat's electric motors remained superior. The much larger craft crept up from behind again, but this time Brocker anticipated their move. When Ben threw the helm over, the banana boat was already beginning the turn, too.

At the crest of the swell, the demon figurehead rose high above the stern of the trimaran. Rigid with fear, Jeri watched it come down. It missed crashing onto the port hull by little more than a foot. Forced deeper into the downwind leg of the turn, Ben doubled back with the aid of the engine, jibed, and came to trim again dangerously close to the long barrier reef.

Brocker got the banana boat through its turn more

efficiently this time and lost less than half the distance as before.

"They're still coming!" Jeri shouted.

Ben had thought there was a chance, but now the outlook was grim. The surf ran white, crashing and spilling over the reef to starboard, and he could feel the change in *Trike*'s response as she cut through steep waves where the ocean dragged across the shallows.

He tried angling out to gain sea room, but for each degree he pointed up, there was a price extracted in speed. Finally, there was no alternative but to maintain the broad reach and await the inevitable.

"We're holding!" Jeri said suddenly, digging her fingers into Ben's shoulder with excitement. "We're going faster!"

Ben turned ten degrees and cranked in the sheets, angling seaward while he could. "No, it's the batteries. They're running down!"

"It worked!" Jeri exclaimed, delighted. "The aluminum actually *worked*!"

Trike opened up the lead rapidly, getting so far ahead that the banana boat became obscured in the darkness behind them. And then the generator came to life.

"*Damn!*" Ben said, hearing the generator's engine speed up to a steady drone. "It's running perfectly. The coil wire must be too far from the block to ground out the ignition!"

"Will they be able to catch us?"

"It's a powerful generator," he answered solemnly,

returning *Trike* to a broad reach and maximum speed. "One of SeaCon's best."

The sound of the generator hung behind them, persisting, growing louder. Then the banana boat became visible again, charging through the sea, closing more rapidly than ever.

"It *is* a demon!" Jeri said through her teeth.

Nothing was going to work this time. No sudden maneuver, no tricks with the wind. The hybrid boat was moving so fast as it bore down on them that it planed crudely.

"The way that thing's running, the batteries have got to be boiling off hydrogen by now," Ben said, clenching one hand into a fist. "Without the exhaust fans to vent it, all we need is one spark, just one — "

The banana boat exploded.

Less than a hundred feet behind them, the sides of the hull were blasted outward, the debris spraying in both directions across the sea. The deck bucked skyward, broke and folded, collapsing. Where there had once been a demon ship, there were now only chunks and pieces of a boat, rising and falling with the swells.

Dropping sails, Ben and Jeri turned back under power of the auxiliary, cautiously approaching the flotsam. Jeri stood at *Trike*'s lifeline and swung the beam of a flashlight over the wreckage.

"Could they still be alive?"

A moan was their answer, followed by a cry for help. Jeri moved the light quickly and found them. The two men, stunned and bruised, were clinging to the demonic figurehead. Ben circled, making certain there was no fight left in them.

Jeri was untying the inflatable to throw to them when the droning of twin diesels approached. A powerful searchlight cut through the darkness and was followed immediately by flashing lights and the wail of a siren.

"It's the patrol boat from Rotole!" she said excitedly.

Within minutes, the U.S. surplus gunboat, engines burbling, lay within fifty feet of the trimaran. Joe Matta and Jeri's father appeared at the rail beside members of the boat's crew.

"Ahoy there!" Vernon Collins called. "Are you all right?"

Jeri waved, laughing with relief. "We're fine, but there are a couple of other people here who could use a lift."

Twenty

Joe Matta's investigation was thorough, and for a few days it dominated Jeri's and Ben's lives.

They learned that Matta had been informed of the existence of the electrically powered banana boat by some Laudat youngsters and had had it under surveillance. When Matta saw that the banana boat was missing on the same night that Mr. Collins came to him concerned because Jeri and Ben had not returned from their diving exploration, he was convinced that a run up the coast in the island's patrol boat was warranted.

The tiny, and normally empty, Sabadoan jail bulged with prisoners. Luckily for the two men in the banana boat, the craft's decking had been stronger than its hull and the main force of the explosion had been deflected away from them. Of their injuries, the most serious remained the Sabadoan's dog bites, for which he was receiving antibiotics. Also in jail were two other local men, a lesser SeaCon employee who was an assistant to Brocker, and Fitzgerald, who promptly confessed everything he knew — and he knew *everything*.

Henri Morgeaux was the creator and head of the operation. A long-time Mayan art buff, Morgeaux had come across the paper by the University of Texas graduate student in the library at Rotole and ultimately followed it to the discovery of the underground portion of the ruins. As a SeaCon attorney who frequented the construction site of the deep-water port in Sabado, he was in a position that made it easy to set up a gang of smugglers and looters.

Morgeaux was now in jail in Guadeloupe, where nearly all of the stolen glyphs had been discovered at a dockside warehouse and where he was trying fancy legal maneuvers to avoid being arraigned on serious charges of importation of stolen art objects.

The apprehension of the looters, along with the discovery of the incredible underground labyrinth of ancient glyphs, caused a tremendous stir locally, as was to be expected, but the electronic age spread the news worldwide as well. Dr. Winston Moore, who as a student had written the paper that Henri Morgeaux and Jeri read, was now head of the anthropology department at the University of Texas. Immediately came his request, which was granted, for permission to gather a team of experts and scholars and conduct a preliminary study of the great archaeological find.

So it went, one thing after another. A group of

SeaCon executives flew in, occupying much of Vernon Collins's time and even some of Jeri's. The executives were especially pleased that the daughter of their project manager had been involved in stopping a horrible wrong that was being done to the island. They thought it was "good for public relations." They did not comment on the fact that it had been SeaCon employees who had initiated the wrong.

* * *

Jeri was at the market in Rotole, hurriedly purchasing items that Anja had requested, when she saw the executives' private plane climbing away from the island. Thinking that now was the chance to catch her father alone, she went directly to the construction site, where she was told he had gone home.

Turning into their drive, she found him walking along the stone pathway that wound among the giant ferns. She got out and joined him. He greeted her with the hug that always made her feel warm and secure.

"So," he said.

"Ben's leaving, Daddy."

He nodded. "He's been leaving since the first day he came, hasn't he?"

"Yes, I suppose so."

"Going in search of himself, is he?"

Jeri laughed. "Maybe. But I think he knows himself pretty well already, and if there's more of him to find, I imagine it'll turn out to be quality stuff."

Vernon Collins looked at his daughter and sighed.

"I imagine so, too." He turned away suddenly and started walking. Jeri followed. "You know, your mother would have loved it here," he said.

One of the daily showers had drifted through earlier, and everything was still dripping. Nearby was an old fence row. The posts had rooted and become trees.

"She loved to watch things grow," he continued. "That's why she wanted you: to watch you grow. Only it didn't work out like that for her, and after she died, I was terrified at the prospect of having to raise you alone. What did I know about such a thing?"

"Only everything," Jeri said, slipping her arm around him and putting her head against his shoulder as they walked.

He laughed. "All I did was see that you were fed and clothed and housed."

"And loved," she added.

"And then it was done. You were grown up before I even knew it."

"Daddy, I keep wanting to go with him. He hasn't asked, but he will if I let him know I'm willing."

Her father stopped and looked at her. "What about college?"

Jeri looked down at the ground. "I know. What about college? What about my life? What about your life? And Ben's? What about Ben's life?" She sighed. "Why is everything so *complicated* all of a sudden?"

"Deep questions," he said softly.

"I don't know what to do," she said, looking up at him. "What should I do?"

Vernon Collins smiled and put his arm around her.

"It's not my decision to make," he said.

* * *

Jeri and Ben slipped the mooring lines from the pilings a few minutes after dawn, as soon as there was enough light to safely navigate the narrow channel out of Humpback Bay. The land breeze and an outgoing tide pulled *Trike* slowly away from the dock.

Ben stood on the deck of the trimaran's port hull with Black Dog beside him. As the space between them widened, Black Dog looked across to Jeri and wagged the stump of his tail.

"You'll write," Jeri said from the dock.

"At every stop," Ben promised.

"And you'll let me know in plenty of time where you'll be at Christmas? So I can fly there over the holidays?"

Ben nodded. "I'll make it the best place I can find by then."

Trike's main and jib filled with air as Ben ran them up, and the trimaran surged ahead smartly. From the cockpit, he drew the sheets taut, and the speed of the multihull jumped again, the craft moving quickly for the open sea.